Fire
&
Ice

A Novel

Megan W. Roma

Some say the world will end in fire,
Some say in ice.
From what I've tasted of desire
I hold with those who favor fire.
But if it had to perish twice,
I think I know enough of hate
To say that for destruction ice
Is also great
And would suffice.

--*Robert Frost,* Fire and Ice

*

Dedicated to my loving spouse, E.H.A., my inspiration for this story.

*

Chapter 1

Fire

"Guys suck."

Maybe it was the overly stuffy, hot, mid-June afternoon. Or possibly it was just because too many things had gone wrong, and all in the span of one day.

Skye Larson sat passenger side in a black 2019 BMW X2, trying to get comfortable, despite her right arm in a sling, and right foot in a cramped boot. Her best friend, Sage Rollins, tailed a blue and white tow truck along I-90, east through Coeur d'Alene, Idaho. The truck carried the crumpled remains of Skye's beloved red 2018 BMW M3, courtesy of her ex-boyfriend.

"Dad won't let me press charges," Skye continued. "So Darrell gets off scot-free." Turmoil raged within.

Sage's mouth unhinged as her eyes narrowed. "What?" she demanded, far louder than their cramped space required.

"After what he pulled? Totally not fair. I know a doc who'll castrate him."

Skye folded her arms and snorted. "If only that easy. But like I said, guys *suck*. So," she added, as her tone softened and wavered. "I'm done with them." She shook her head slightly. "Forever."

Except that tall, cute, blond-haired guy hitchhiking about a mile back had caught her eye. It wasn't without focused effort that she pushed him out of her mind.

A slight smile escaped Sage's mouth before she clamped it. "Skye Larson throws in the towel after two long years of four hormonal boyfriends. That should make the Coeur d'Alene Press cover page."

"Sage, I'm serious!" Skye said, using her best depressed tone. "Look at me! Traumatized arm and foot. Lucky I wasn't killed."

Sage shrugged. "Okay, you need some fun on your first day out of the house in like, for-ev-er. We drop off Caesar, then off to Marmalade's. I need a new top. Or do we want coffee first?"

Skye's light brown eyebrows arched uncannily high. "You have to ask? Coffee is life."

"Just checking to see if you're still in there." She paused. "Caesar *is* a boy's name," she teased. "You gotta change it if you're giving them up."

Skye scowled. "Never. That car is perfect. Was perfect." She groaned. "I'm gonna kill Darrell!"

"Just remember," Sage soothed, "if you're going cold turkey, you can't kill them, either. Unfortunate, but a rule."

"It's a stupid rule."

"Okay, let's change the subject. Remember I'm trying to cheer you up."

A wry smile passed along Skye's lips. "Try harder."

"Right then." Sage switched on the radio as a commercial was ending.

"...*we do it right the first time,*" came a friendly masculine voice through the Bose car speakers. *"Max's Auto Body Shop, located at 415 Auto Park Road, just off I-90. Open 8-to-5-week days. 10 to 4 on Saturdays."*

As Taylor Swift's *ME!* blasted through the car speakers, Sage glanced over.

"Isn't that where we're going? Max's?"

Skye nodded and added a roll of the eyes. "Yup. My dad can't say enough about that place. *Max has the best guys in town—*

8

why heck, they can fix anything!" She mimicked a low voice and peered again at her wrecked M3. "They better not mess up my baby."

"Too late for that."

"You know what I mean."

The tow truck took the Auto Park Road exit off the I-90 freeway. Sage followed it to Auto Park Road.

Skye gestured. "There it is. On the left, by Los Jalapeños."

"Yep, I see it. Hope they're still open."

"Should be," Skye said, looking at her phone. "It's only 4:58."

The blue and white tow truck remained in the safety zone as thick oncoming traffic powered by.

Skye sighed. "Must be rush hour."

More cars, along with another minute. Then more cars. Skye stared at the *Reliable Towing* insignia beneath her BMW another full minute before the truck turned a quick left onto the gravel parking lot. Sage followed close behind, acting like the tail end of the tow truck, just as the next group of cars approached. Two oncoming trucks slammed on their brakes and honked, as a guy in one of them waved at her with a single finger.

Sage parked behind the tow after it stopped. "See?" she proclaimed with a sparkling smile. "Delivered you all safe and sound!"

Skye just managed to avoid another eye roll as she looked at the unimpressive garage in front of them: two-story, beige and brown, with white trim. Four garage bays took up the bottom floor, with two doors presently open. The second story looked like someone's apartment, with a huge square window front and center.

"I'm trusting my baby to this dump?" she fumed, snatching an envelope from her purse. "Well, let's get this over with."

The husky tow driver hopped out of her truck and met a short man who emerged from the shop. He stood stocky, with a nicely trimmed black beard and a dark blue jump suit bearing the name *Max*. As the two shook hands, Skye limped up to Max and handed him the envelope.

"This is from my dad," she said. She pointed hopefully to her dead M3. "Can you fix it?"

Max scanned the letter and nodded in acknowledgement. As the driver released the crushed M3 and drove away, Max's eyes grew large. He walked around the car with the speed of a half-dead turtle. His face appeared far more serious and much less optimistic than Skye would have hoped.

"Let me get our expert," he said quietly. "Be right back." He disappeared into one of the open bay doors.

"That doesn't sound good," Sage said quietly. "Isn't he Max, of Max's Auto Body Shop?"

"Shh-h-h, he'll hear you," Skye murmured. "If he says he has an expert, all the better."

A moment later Skye's world seemed to stop, and not in a good way. Following Max was a guy who looked around her age. About 6' 2", handsome as a movie star and ripped—his muscles bulged through his shirt. This added to his black hair and square jawline amounted to someone who seemed uncomfortably familiar.

"Is that...Darrell?" Sage whispered a second before Skye did.

"Maybe his twin?" Skye guessed.

It was uncanny, but no, Skye told herself. Darrell—who was strung up in the hospital ward with two broken arms, two broken legs, four cracked ribs and a full-blown concussion, had no siblings. And this beefcake in front of her wore a snake tattoo down his well-muscled right arm. Darrell always dissed guys with skin markings or piercings of any kind.

The hunk walked confidently over to the wrecked M3 and examined it inside and out, without introducing himself to Skye. He studied the crumpled body, the smashed-out windows, and damaged seats.

"This is Dorran, our auto body specialist," Max said, as the young man knelt and ran his hands carefully over the side fenders, the hood, and doors.

"What... *happened*?" Dorran murmured, loud enough for Skye to hear. He grimaced and whistled as he looked under the car and finally, the roof before siding back up to Max. "The thing is beyond totaled," he said, matter of fact. "End of story."

Skye glared at him, ticked at being ignored. "Hello? Over here? You know? Car owner?"

Dorran's eyes quickly took in Skye's face, her arm in a sling, and finally her boot. His face softened.

"You're lucky to be alive!" he said with a slight smile. His voice was low, masculine. Sexy. But his words, along with his annoying resemblance to her ex-boyfriend, set her off.

"Oh, really?" she snapped. "Would that be your expert opinion? Just tell me if you can fix the car!"

Dorran's expression turned a 180. "Surprise me, please. Say something intelligent," he said. "That *is* anyone's expert opinion when you look at that. Your insurance won't cover the damages to repair. It would be cheaper to buy something else. A lot cheaper."

Skye eyed the mechanic, impressed by his ability to fight back. Darrell would have just collapsed like a wet noddle. But she wasn't going to give up.

"I don't want another car!" she retorted, her right arm suddenly flaring with pain. "Are you really a skilled mechanic or just a moron trying to impress?"

"Not too many people like you, do they?" Dorran shot back smoothly, as if he'd practiced that line before. He looked at her with an upraised eyebrow.

Skye felt her face flush as Sage gripped her shoulder. "Chill out," she counseled.

"Yeah, I know," Skye replied, massaging her throbbing arm. But her eyes bore into Dorran, and she watched as he looked over the letter Max offered. She overheard the words *self-insured*, as she limped over and leaned on her first car ever. The one possession she could really call her own, no strings attached. The thing she wasn't going to let go of. No. Matter. What.

A moment later the dark-haired hunk took another slow and careful look at the mangled red BMW, while distancing himself from Skye. Max followed and together they forced the crumpled hood open.

"Engine looks mostly intact," Max said, scratching his beard. "A new radiator, grill and compressor, hoses. Some under body work. Not a whole lot else. So it's mostly you."

Skye watched as Dorran closed his eyes and sighed audibly. He glared quickly at Skye, then at the car again. He turned to Max, folded his arms, and said one only word.

"Okay."

Sage nudged Skye forward.

"What?" Skye snapped at her, looking to Dorran. "It's not like he's doing me any favors." She shrugged. "I'm not even convinced he can do the job right. We should go somewhere else."

Dorran smiled darkly, unfolded his arms and looked at Max. "Now that's the most intelligent thing she's said so far. She should go—somewhere else."

Skye's eyes widened and Sage snorted. Max stepped forward.

"Miss Larson," he began with a placating smile. "No one else—and I mean *no one,* would ever touch this car—that I can guarantee. Maybe you could salvage some of it for parts." He paused, looking at Dorran quickly. "But the reason why we're even willing to consider taking this on is because your father does a lot of business with us. And this *skilled mechanic,* can do it if anyone can. He's the best I have ever seen in my twenty plus years in the business."

Skye leaned forward, eyes blazing at the hunk. "And how is that supposed to make me feel?"

Dorran shifted and started to walk off. "People like her are why I get ulcers, Max. I don't need this."

Max shrugged at Skye. "Last chance, Miss Larson. He'll do you right."

Skye's inner fire cooled a little. She took another glance at her car, convinced Max was telling the truth. Her one opportunity was slipping away.

"Okay," she said with a sigh. "Please fix my car."

Dorran stopped in his tracks and turned around, seemingly amused she agreed to the job.

"How long is this going to take?" Skye asked. "A couple of weeks?"

"Your misguided opinion is false, but cute," Dorran said.

Max stifled a laugh. "No, Miss Larson," he said. "I would estimate six to eight weeks. At least."

"Two...months." Her face betrayed her surprise as she tried to imagine herself without wheels for that long.

"You're basically talking about a new car," Max explained as Dorran stepped forward, apparently ready to toss her another insult. "We have to inventory all the parts, get the orders in to various warehouses around the globe, make sure everything comes in as it should. Most of the time at least some parts have to be returned. And lastly, a new paint job." He looked at Skye as if to appeal. "You sure you don't want to just buy a new car?"

"Nope," Skye said as she shook her head. Anger welled within. She knew they wouldn't understand. They couldn't. But not wanting to prolong the awkward moment, she signaled Sage and they retreated back to her car.

Sage started up her BMW and looked at Skye.

"That could have gone...better."

"I'm protective of Caesar," Skye said defensively. "You know that."

"Hmmm. What do you think of the hunky mechanic? Still vowing to swear off men?"

"More than ever. That guy was off-the-charts rude. I hope he treats his cars better than his customers." She paused. "But at least he's got a backbone."

"He's got a lot more than that," Sage murmured as she looked in her rearview mirror. "Did you see the way he studied Caesar? Like someone figuring out a puzzle. Anyway, let's find a Dutch Bros."

"Amen to that," Skye agreed.

Chapter 2
Ice

Finn Parker whistled as he emerged from the shop. The tall, slim, and handsome mechanic sauntered over in his greasy tan overalls. Both were 21, but Finn's stringy dirt blonde hair and blue cap covered most of his face and head, in contrast to Dorran's clean-cut look. And Dorran stood about two inches taller.

"That's what I call one fiery chick," Finn said.

Dorran's eyebrows shot up. "You gonna help me finish putting the glass on the Camaro or daydream about the millionaire's daughter?" Finn half-heartedly glared at Dorran, but followed him back inside.

In the second bay they replaced the front windshield of a classy blue and white 1968 Chevy Camaro. After applying the urethane, they lowered the glass slowly in place, after which Dorran studied the seams and glass for any imperfections. After about five minutes (Finn timed him), he gave his final approval after shifting the windshield slightly into its final position.

Dorran wiped his hands on a grease rag. "How come you didn't give me any backup out there?" he asked with a wry smile. "Assisting with obnoxious and unbearable customers is in your job description, right Max?" he added over his shoulder.

"That's right," Max called from under a faded red Volkswagen Bug. "All for one, that sort of thing."

Finn laughed. "It looked like you handled her barbs in your conventionally sick way. In fact, I think she was starting to flirt."

"Hardly a seduction," Dorran replied. "Besides, Rule Number One, remember? Don't date the customer's daughter."

"Good idea," Max called out again as he rolled his shop creeper from beneath the Bug. He pointed his SAE wrench at Finn. "You can learn a few things from this boy."

"C'mon Max!" Finn called back, half teasing. "It was one time and she was like, way older!"

"Yeah," Dorran joked. "By a whoppin' twenty-three days."

Finn stiffened, a smile growing. "She told me she didn't care. Anyway, since

Skye's boyfriend is in the hospital, maybe she's, you know," he shrugged. "Available."

"Did she look *available* to you, Mr. Steal-Your-Girl?" Dorran asked, his right eyebrow raised.

Finn shrugged. "Worth taking a shot, right?" he added quietly, his face coloring. "Anyway, word on the street is she dumped Darrell."

"Tell you what," Dorran said with a gleam in his eye. "You take this project on. Cherry out that wreck—" he pointed to the red heap outside— "and win her heart. A win-win all around."

"Ha-ha." Finn frowned. "I don't have the expertise," he said casually. "But you might give her a chance."

"I don't date princesses. Her dad is big time in this town and I'm not getting mixed up in that." He looked at Finn. "Let's roll the beast into bay three."

"I'll help," Max offered, emerging from beneath the Bug. "And it's past closing time. You guys up for some OT?"

"I'm hanging out at Paddy's tonight," Finn said. He glanced at Dorran. "Happy hour 'til six."

"I'm hitting the trail with Trey after I order a book for this...this." He looked at the wreckage and grimaced. "Project."

Although Skye Larson's car was in neutral with the brake disengaged, only two of the wheels would move on the BMW. As the three pushed, pulled and swore at the crumpled M3, it left a rubber trail in its wake.

Before long, a high-pitched whine of a motorcycle barreled up the street. Trey Hunter, a blonde, stocky and chiseled twenty-something, hopped off his Harley Low Rider and jumped in to join the tug of war. With his help, a few more minutes of struggle secured the BMW safely inside the bay.

Trey looked the wrecked car over. "Not much to part out," he observed, looking first to Max then at Dorran. "What do you want it for?"

Dorran gave a forced smile. "A rebuild," he said sardonically. "Custom order."

Trey's eyebrows shot skyward. "You got some special magic in there or what?"

"Remains to be seen," Dorran replied as he washed at the sink. "So what say we grab some food at Roger's before we go?"

Trey nodded. "Sounds good."

"You remember the paperwork?"

"Of course. Last time was a glitch. Let it go."

Dorran watched Max give Finn a knowing look without saying anything. He felt his face grow hot as he walked his '69 Honda CB750 from a corner of the shop and into the hot summer air.

Dorran and Trey stopped off at Roger's Ice Cream and Burgers on Sherman Avenue. They picked up Triple-D burgers and Cokes before cruising out of town and turning onto East French Gulch Road.

The sun still sat high on this very warm June afternoon as they wove their way along the rural route of fenced-in fields, small clusters of conifers and the occasional mailbox or driveway. The speed limit of 35 always seemed laughable to Dorran, who revved his bike to 60. Yet he eyed the unevenly paved road carefully, always on the lookout for potholes or deer. A voice inside warned him that someday his luck might run out.

But he pushed that worry aside and breathed deeply, taking in the fresh smell of pine as he sped along, savoring the freedom. He loved this route, with its picturesque scenery and open spaces. He often thought how he might eventually buy a place out here, though that was little more than a pipe dream. But after tonight it wasn't even going to be that.

Dorran eyed the benign cirrus clouds as they slowed onto East Fernan Hill Road, with its 25 MPH signs, numerous houses, and small *slow down* signs, warning drivers of kids, dogs, cats, birds and ducklings. The richly mixed landscape of browning fields and woods met them until the deep blue Fernan Lake came into view. About two miles later, Dorran took a left onto a partially concealed dirt path.

He shut off his bike and parked on a flat browning meadow, with its grand view of blue water, rimmed with green conifers. Seconds later Trey joined him, and together they hiked down the hill that turned rocky. The trail ended on a shaded cliff, looking over the expansive lake.

As Dorran sat and pulled a burger out of his bag, he gestured at the water. "So, what do you think?"

Trey laughed with wide eyes as he took in the scenery. "This is sick! I never knew this place even existed."

"Most people don't, and I won't be advertising."

"How did you find it?"

"A customer," Dorran began. "Liked my work. We started talking about the outdoors. He invited me out here and I was hooked. Said I could come out whenever."

"This *is* the life," Trey agreed as he pulled out his food.

Dorran considered his words, but couldn't exactly embrace the concept. At least not yet. Something wild stirred inside him: an untamed, restless energy refusing to settle down to a status quo. Even here in paradise.

"I could get used to this," Trey said before taking a bite. "It's a great escape."

"Something like that," Dorran agreed quietly. "I have to get out of that town or I'll go crazy. Being in the shop all day…" He trailed off with a shrug.

"I hear you," Trey replied. "The office can get insane. Some days, hardly any business, and other times." He shook his head. "I wonder where they all come from."

Dorran looked over the placid lake, with its boaters, fishermen, water-skiers and kayakers. A few jet-skied on the lake's western edge, leaving a temporary white trail behind them. He felt a sense of longing to be down there in the middle of all that action and fun. And his impatience scolded him: life *was* passing him by. He knew he could never have anyone like Skye, so why even entertain that thought? He'd never be accepted into their society, no matter how much he wanted it.

"So you still want to sign up?"

Trey's voice pulled him away from his gloomy thoughts. Dorran nodded slowly as he took a bite.

"Yeah."

Trey leaned back on his hands, his mouth twisting. "I know I'm not supposed to ask this, Dorran, but off the record, why? It seems you have a good setup with Max. Comfortable apartment above the shop, walk only a few feet to work. The pay is good."

Dorran grit his teeth. "It's dead-end. I'm stuck. I'm 21 and want to see the world. No family yet so I suppose this is my chance. I only have a GED and no college, so my options are limited. Figure I can get some training and branch out."

"You won't make nearly as much for a long time," Trey said quietly. "You get housing allowance or you can stay on base, but not much else."

"Not worried about money," Dorran said with a wry smile. "But isn't there medical?"

Trey deadpanned. "Of course."

Dorran snorted. "And they call you a recruiter?"

Trey shrugged. "I also look at what's a good fit, not just someone desperate to go elsewhere, or running away from his or her past life."

Dorran shot him a glare.

"I'm not running away."

Trey eyed him a moment and shrugged. "Not saying you are, but some do. There are good career moves in the service, and you might even earn a college degree eventually—if that's what you want. Your juvey record is still being reviewed, but from what I've heard, it won't disqualify you. You passed the ASVAB, and your physical got final approval yesterday. So you're good to go."

Trey pulled an envelope from his pack and handed it over. He offered Dorran a pen with bold red letters that said GO ARMY on one side. The other side said BEAT NAVY.

"Here's your enlistment," Trey said. "Just read carefully before you sign. Any questions, just ask. I already filled in the parts we talked about."

After Dorran read the contract thoroughly—all four pages worth, Trey continued.

"I checked you off for a delayed enlistment, but there's no guarantee when you'll be shipped out."

"Any guess would help," Dorran said.

"My best guess? Early to mid-August."

Dorran thought out loud. "That should work. I still have some projects to finish before I go. Can't leave Max in a lurch—especially with today's new surprise."

"You mean that crumpled heap of metal?"

"Yep, courtesy of Skye Larson."

Trey whistled. "I heard about the rollover."

Dorran looked at him wryly. "Just another pleasure ride gone wrong, if you ask me."

Trey smiled. "And Skye Larson. What a catch she would be. She's pretty cute."

Dorran wagged his head. "Maybe, once she gets clear of her bruised face and attitude. You'll have to compete with Finn, though. He wants a shot."

Trey raised his palms. "Out of my league and too hot for me. Her father has serious connections with the military so I won't even entertain that notion." He paused. "And I hear she can be a hard pill to swallow."

Dorran snorted. "That's putting it mildly." He smiled remembering the insults she threw at him. "But I need to finish her car before I ship out."

Trey nodded. "There are no guarantees. I just send the application along with the notes."

Dorran took the pen in hand, signed and dated the form, and offered it to Trey.

"Not going to think it over?" Trey asked.

Dorran shook his head and pushed the papers and pen at him. "No. I'm up for it," he said.

"When you're ready, stop by the MEPS so we can swear you in. That's all there is to it."

Dorran nodded, feeling a thrill at all the possibilities. A step into the great unknown and the adventures that waited for him.

Chapter 3
Fire

Skye shut Sage's car door and waved as her best friend slowly drove away from the Larson estate. As the BMW exited the expansive metal gates, Skye felt a twinge of jealousy at the loss of her freedom. Realizing the regaining of that autonomy depended on a young car mechanic who seemed less than excited to take on the task, enveloped her into a depression.

Skye hefted her Marmalade's shopping bag, limped over to the large red and black brick fountain, and sat on its wide edge. She watched the clear water shoot into the air like miniature fireworks before descending softly back to the pool below. Her thoughts drifted to a summer of yesteryear when she swam in it—one of the finest memories of this place, until Wallace the butler dragged her out of the water and subsequently scolded her for several long minutes.

Her shoulders drooped. Only a week out of college saw her car wrecked and her social status changed to single. Not that losing Darrell was a tragedy, since he was only a handsome clone of the other three loser boyfriends over the past two years. Why was it so hard to find someone who wasn't always trying to get into her pants? Was she nothing more than a commodity to be exploited?

Inwardly she pushed away a rush of anger as she pressed her phone button—almost 7 o'clock. Dinner would have started by now, though she didn't feel hungry or motivated to step inside the Larson mansion. She wished the stars were out so she would have an excuse to stay longer, but June never turned dark that early.

The soft sounds of shoes caused Skye's head to swivel.

"Good evening, miss," came the voice of one of the housemaids. Short, dark hair and medium build, she was one of Skye's favorites.

Skye smiled at her soft British accent. "Hi Molly," she replied. "I suppose I'm late for dinner."

"Wallace did send me to fetch you," she said hopefully.

Skye sighed. "Fine, I'm coming."

"Can I take that bag?" Molly offered. "Looks heavy."

She stood and handed it over. "Thanks," she said. "Just some new clothes."

As Skye limped toward the mansion, she mentally prepared for dinner with her father and mother, Charles and Adelaide Larson. *Breathe, relax, smile,* she reminded herself. *Breathe, relax, smile. You can do this.*

Molly eyed her carefully as they started up the mansion's entryway steps.

"You feeling all right, Miss?" she asked carefully, her face taking on a slight look of worry.

Skye sighed. "Long day," she replied. "I think my pain pills are wearing off."

"I'll see that your prescription is refilled if you wish," she offered politely.

Skye nodded slightly. "Thank you."

"Of course."

The grand entry doors opened before them, where a short black man awaited, dressed as an elegant butler with a head of silvering hair. His dazzling white smile made Skye wish she wore sunglasses.

"Another beautiful evening, Miss Larson," he said cheerfully.

"I suppose," she replied wistfully. "What's up, Wallace?" she asked.

"We await your presence for dinner."

Skye stopped and snorted. "Really, Wallace?" she teased. "Who talks like that? *We await your presence for dinner.*" She mimicked in a low voice.

"Nevertheless," he replied, his eyes narrowing slightly. "Your father and mother are waiting. For you. In the dining hall."

Trouble brewed on the man's face as Skye realized her parents would not eat until she arrived. So she slumped and contorted her face.

"Okay, Wallace," she said, accelerating her limp. "Lead the way."

The man had to hurry to open the tall, chestnut dining hall doors to prevent Skye from slamming into them. She smiled slightly as he appeared to adjust his tie and practice his smile as he walked in to face his employer.

Wallace led the way into the elaborate dining hall, where a long, immaculate table occupied much of the room. Only three settings were placed on the far end. Her father, in his dark business suit, sat at the head, while her mother sat on his left, leaving the one on his right for her.

"Skye," Charles Larson said as he stood tall on his feet. "Glad you could make it." His wife Adelaide stood as well, revealing a V-neck chiffon dinner dress, along with a forced smile.

"Hello Father...Mother," she replied, limping up to them. "Sorry I'm late." They greeted each other with a kiss on the cheek. "Have a good day?"

Charles tilted his gray head. "Like any other I suppose." He eyed her carefully. "You seem a little pale tonight. Are you feeling all right?"

"Like any other day I suppose," she returned with a slight smile as they sat.

Wallace stood a few feet away, ramrod straight, and cleared his throat. "Tonight's main selection is crab-stuffed lobster tail," he announced. "Clam chowder or shrimp salad as your appetizers and strawberry shortcake for dessert."

"Very good Wallace," Charles replied. "I will have the chowder."

"Chowder for me as well," Adelaide said. She smiled at Skye with her ruby red lips.

"Shrimp salad," she replied in turn.

Wallace nodded slightly. "Very good," he said as he turned and left for the kitchen.

Adelaide looked to her husband, her total attention focused on him. Skye noticed a few more wrinkles on her forehead she hadn't seen before.

"How was your day, dear?" she asked.

"Mixed," came his reply, his large hands twitching. "The DOW was up only 62 points and the S&P down five. The NASDAQ fell 15 at the bell."

"How did our stocks do, Father?" Skye asked in a gentle, practiced voice.

Charles beamed at her through his steely gray eyes. "Well enough," he said. "This has been a good month for us—in fact a good year, so the day-to-day fluctuations don't amount to much in the big scheme of things."

As Wallace served the appetizers, Mr. Larson summarized the daily mortgage and bond rates. This was where Skye tuned out, so she focused on her shrimp salad and reflected on her first encounter with Dorran, who looked so much like her ex-boyfriend it hardly seemed a coincidence. Could they be related?

After several more minutes of financial details, Mr. Larson turned to Adelaide.

"And how was your day?" he asked.

Skye's mother lit up as she placed her spoon inside her soup bowl. She sat up straight and patted her loosely braided blond hair with her right hand.

"Arrowroot's permits were approved today. Mike wants to start within a couple of days."

Charles beamed at her. "Stone Construction is a good company. I knew you could do it." He looked at her proudly. "You have the makings of a tycoon, you know."

Adelaide laughed gently at his praise. "I don't know about that," she said as her face colored. "But that is all the news I have."

Charles turned his attention to his daughter.

"And now Skye?" he asked. "Tell us about your day. Did everything go well at the auto shop?" He looked at his wife. "Isn't Max's right across the street from your new bakery?"

Adelaide nodded.

Skye took a deep breath and swallowed as her heart sped up.

"It went well enough, Father," she answered calmly. "The car, unfortunately, is a total wreck and it may take up to two months before it is completely repaired."

Charles nodded. "That is understandable considering the damage."

"Which leaves me without transportation for the summer," Skye continued, still maintaining her composure.

"We will see to that," Charles reassured her. "Wallace or Marcus can drive you around until you are well enough. Then you can choose a rental until your car is ready."

Wallace entered the dining hall with plates of crab-stuffed lobster tail. Skye waited patiently until everyone was served and Wallace disappeared behind the side doors.

"And I did have a question," Skye said.

"Of course," her father said, looking mildly surprised. "You can always talk to me about anything. What is it?"

"I was wondering," Skye began, trying a pensive look. "If it might not be better to pursue legal action against Darrell—after he is released from the hospital and allowed to recover, of course. Because if he is allowed to take advantage of every—"

Charles held up his hand, shutting Skye down.

"We've already discussed this," he said. "Darrell's family are good friends. They have formally apologized and even agreed to pay for all the damages to your car. Besides, Darrell's injuries are more serious than yours. He has suffered enough."

Though appeased that Darrell's family would pay her car bills, Skye still felt a pulse of annoyance at her father's dismissive approach. But past experience told her there was nothing more to say, so she retained her mask and smiled.

"How is Darrell, by the way?" she asked in a polite tone.

Mr. and Mrs. Larson looked at each other briefly, before Charles nodded to his wife.

"He hasn't regained consciousness," she said. "The doctors think he may have suffered some brain trauma." She looked at Skye. "More tests are needed though."

Serves him right, Skye thought to herself, as anger flared within. *Though with his luck he'll be out of the hospital in a few short days.*

"Did we send flowers?" she asked aloud.

Her mother nodded. "And I wrote a card for you, expressing your sympathy."

Both parents looked at her expectantly as Skye's stomach revolted, threatening an immediate release. But she managed to keep perfect composure. "Good," she replied. "I hope he feels better soon."

"I understand if you break up with Darrell," her father added. "By the way, a few young men from work have specifically asked about you. Maybe we can invite them over."

"Who?" she asked, trying to keep her tone in check.

Charles furrowed his brows and stared into space. "Why, there's Gerald Astor, or Richard Livingston, Elon Chanler, and even Mark Cushing."

"I don't recall any of them," Skye admitted, though she wasn't looking forward to meeting anyone at this point. Like she promised Sage, she was done.

"Most have finished their schooling and are working their way up through the bank," her father said proudly." He looked in her direction. "And of course the bank misses you," he said. "Did the doctor say when you could return to work?"

"Now Charles," Adelaide interrupted smoothly, as if on cue. "Skye has at least two more weeks before the boot comes off. Then her physician will consider how she is mending."

"Oh yes, of course," the man said with a smile. "But don't worry about money, Skye.

Your weekly allowance will always be there for you."

"Thank you," she said sweetly.

The three ate in silence until Charles finished his plate and called for the strawberry dessert. When half of her dessert was in Skye's stomach, she spoke again.

"There is something else," she began, maintaining a professional tone.

"Yes?" Charles replied. His eyebrows shot up though his focus remained on his dessert.

"About school," she said pleasantly, her heart now pounding loudly in her chest. How her father or mother could not hear it was beyond her. "I was thinking about changing my major."

Her father stopped eating and her mother's fork dropped to her plate with a *clang*.

Charles cleared his throat. "It isn't uncommon for young people to change their career paths," he began. "But yours has been carefully thought out. With an economics major you are easily able to stay within the family business. You could be a research market analyst, an economic consultant, a financial analyst—heck, even a lawyer!" He spoke as if giving a rehearsed speech to shareholders: smooth and convincing. "What would you consider to be a proper choice?" he asked.

"Advertising," she replied evenly.

Skye and Adelaide watched as Mr. Larson seemed to weigh this in his mind.

"And what would you do with this degree?" he asked.

"Advertising majors can be in copywrite, graphic design, managing web sites, marketing, media buyers, account executives, product managers," she said, knowing he was well aware of the answer. "The list goes on."

Her father nodded approvingly.

"And the salary?" he pressed.

"It varies."

"Indeed it does," he said, setting his fork on his plate. "You might make only a third in advertising as you would otherwise." He paused, looking her in the eye. "How about a minor in advertising?"

Skye smiled. "How about a minor in economics?"

Charles laughed and wiped his mouth with his napkin before he spoke. "I would like a little more research from you before I make a decision. Draw up a proposal for my review and we will discuss it."

Adelaide laughed. "Dear, you sound like a bank CEO instead of your daughter's father."

He looked at her with a benign smile. "I am both of those things." But a thought seemed to strike him and he pointed at Skye. "Help your mother with Arrowroot this summer instead of working at the bank," he said. "Take the advertising lead. If you are successful, well..." He smiled. "And you can keep an eye on that car of yours at the same time."

Skye could hardly believe her father's words. This was a dream come true. A thrill ran through her as she thought about this opportunity, but she managed to keep it controlled, just like her other emotions. She looked her father in the eye.

"All right," she said with a slight smile. "And I'll show you what I can do."

The man laughed. "I look forward to it."

Chapter 4
Ice

As Max's Autobody neared closing time on a muggy Thursday afternoon, Dorran bent over the computer keyboard for the hundredth time. With sweat dripping down his face, he watched as the view screen showed only the slightest fraction of a bent frame. The young mechanic was so close he could taste it. One more iteration would do it.

After he made the final adjustments in the computer, he rechecked the brackets and clamps mounted on the pinch welds before hitting "enter" on the keyboard.

The automotive frame machine hummed as the chains wrenched the completely stripped-out-car slightly to the left. After thirty more seconds, the machine stopped and Dorran checked the results.

Right on target.

Dorran sat on the register stool with a huge sigh. Finn came up and slapped his back.

"Congrats! Now you get the fun part," he said with a laugh. "Welding."

"Don't remind me," Dorran replied, his energy level now cratering.

Max leaned in and studied the screen for a moment. He whistled softly.

"You do the impossible, Dorran. Great job." He looked at the sweating mechanic. "Now get out of here. It's closing time."

*

After taking a shower and grabbing a quick bite, Dorran pulled his Honda from the back of the shop. As he locked the door and emerged onto the parking lot, so did a long black limousine.

Dorran swore, fairly certain of who it would be. "Note to self: next time take a quicker shower."

Skye Larson emerged from the limo, dressed in a brown skirt and white top, this time without a sling supporting her arm. She eyed Dorran with a look of disdain while she powerwalked right up to him.

"Great, the mechanic!" she said abruptly, as her butler brought up the rear.

Dorran swung his right leg over the seat of his bike, his hand inches from the starter.

"Miss Larson," he said evenly, wearing a slight smile. "It is after hours." He looked from the handlebars to her face. He noticed she no longer carried any bruises. "What can I do for you?"

"You can give me an update on my car," she said with a hint of impatience.

Dorran glanced at both Skye and Wallace as he shook his head.

"Well, sorry to tell you Miss Larson, but we're not Walmart. We close at five and you are—" he pulled out his cell phone and pushed a button, "47 minutes past that."

Skye huffed. "So?" she demanded. "I worked today as well. Just got off an hour ago."

Dorran tilted his head. "Not my problem." He was about to start his bike, but she held out her hand.

"I think you can spare an hour to go over what you've done so far," she said, folding her arms back into place. "If anything."

Dorran looked at her, humored. "Only one hour, Miss Larson?" he said in a mocking tone. "Why, nothing would please me more. Why not make it two?" He grinned at her and started his bike. "Come by bright and early tomorrow morning!" he said over the engine's roar. "We open at eight!"

He slid his helmet over his head.

Skye put her hands on her hips and glared.

"You haven't done a thing with it, have you?"

Dorran's smile faded a little as his mind rewound the last several days. But he determined to show none of the annoyance he felt.

"You'll just have to come in and see for yourself."

"Why not tonight?" she pressed. "You're here, I'm here. Let's get this done!"

"Nice sales pitch," Dorran quipped. "But I'll have to pass."

Skye glared at him. "I knew it. You haven't done a thing for my car, have you? You're nothing but a lazy, no good, son of—"

Dorran revved his bike and drove it off the parking lot without saying another word. From his rearview mirror he saw Skye turn on Wallace and yell before giving Dorran the finger.

As Dorran weaved his bike in and out along the shaded road to Fernan Lake, he tried to push Skye's face out of his mind and remind himself to simply enjoy the ride.

He was here.

In this place.

Right now.

It was always too easy to dwell on the negatives of the past instead of enjoying what he had in the present.

He accepted as a fact of life that she would never be satisfied with his work—her initial attitude told him that. After a few years of dealing with customers it was easy to see that coming. Attempting to please her would be like trying to keep his own mom sober. Or make her hang around long enough to raise her son. Just wasn't gonna happen.

As he sat on the cliff overlooking the blue waters of Fernan Lake, he took in a long, deep breath. Tonight the air seemed to carry an unusual sense of calm as it sent a gentle warm wind across his face.

Dorran's thoughts returned again to the enviably rich Skye Larson. He tried to imagine how life would turn out if he never had to worry about buying a place or raising a family on his salary. And of course, there was her family: strong, stable, supportive. Everything he never had.

But he refocused. Miring in self-pity was only self-destructive. He made it this far already, and he had many years ahead of him to show others he would make it in this world.

That he could be worthy.

Someday.

As Dorran made his way back home, the sunset colors of pink and red permeated the western sky. As Dorran's thoughts turned to Finn and Max, his stomach churned as his plans nagged at him, his conscience accusing him of desertion. After everything his friends did to support him when he was desperate, and now he was going to leave. But at least he'd finish out Skye's car, regardless of her obnoxious behavior. And as long as his boss approved of the job, he could care less about what she thought.

As Dorran crawled into his bed, his mind still unsettled with Skye's conduct, he knew sleep was not going to come easy. He picked up his copy of *Automotive Technology* from the bed stand, and started reading where he left off: Chapter 75, Throttle Position Sensors...

*

The shrieking noises of a smoke detector emanated from somewhere above. Eleven-year-old Dorran opened his eyes to thick smoke, red and orange flames, and his own coughing fits. Muffled voices called his name as he sat up. Confusion filled his mind as someone pulled him from his warm bed. A fireman carried him out of his bedroom and into the freezing night air. The boy shivered partly from cold, and more so at being mostly naked. But a kind stranger wrapped a thick blanket around him and led him away from the burning trailer.

*

Dorran jerked up in his queen bed, the jarring sounds of a fire alarm rattling through his brain. But this time the sounds were real, and not from one of his nightmares.

He rolled out of bed, crossed his apartment in record time, and yanked open the door leading to the downstairs and outside of his home. As panic swept through him, he took the stairs three at a time until he reached the bottom level and forced open the door.

"Where's the fire? Where's the fire?" he cried, to no one in particular. His mind was still partly stuck in a dream of smoke and flames.

But someone was there, waiting for him. A smile spread across her face and her eyes took in his entire physique. Skye Larson, dressed in a seamless cami and white Capri pants, ready for the day with coffee cup in hand.

In a flash, Dorran realized he wore nothing but gray boxer briefs. His hands flew down to cover himself as his face heated to lava levels.

"Bright and early, just like you said!" Skye teased. "I tried knocking, but you didn't answer. So..." Her voice trailed off but her eyes never left his body.

Dorran looked around for any hint of smoke or sign of a fire, but neither existed. He frowned at Skye.

"You set off the fire alarm?" he shouted.

"Well...yeah!" she replied. "You think I was going to wait around until you ditch me with another excuse?" She smiled again. "Though I have to say—you give quite a show."

Dorran felt his face prickle.

"You like what you see?" he asked in a low, menacing voice.

Skye shrugged, the self-indulgent smile now seeping from her face. "Maybe. But I was hoping for a car show more than a strip tease."

Dorran pointed his index finger in the air.

"Just a moment," he said, as he retreated inside the building and closed the door. He turned and stood in place, his body shaking slightly as anger continued to mount. He sat on one of the steps, placed his head in his hands and took in a deep breath. His stomach started to hurt. Bad.

He cleared his mind, fighting back thoughts of revenge with all the energy that was inside him. He had to be better than that. But knowing time was short, he forced himself to his feet. An adjacent door on his left led directly into the shop, where he found and turned the shut-off switch for the fire alarm. The blaring noises ceased at once, creating a welcomed but empty silence.

He took a deep breath, and another, bringing his mind back to his pre-nightmare state. He fixated on Fernan Lake. The deep, blue water. Riding his bike down the shady roads. And as he fed his mind these scenes, he felt his entire body slowly relax and his heart rate settle. Once again, he was in complete control of himself.

Decision made, relief swept over Dorran, allowing him to focus. As he reopened the door to the outside, he didn't even bother shielding his underwear with his hands. He looked right into Skye Larson's eyes.

Skye observed his face, her confident smile disappearing as she took a sudden step back.

"What's the matter?" she demanded.

"Miss Larson, you can have your car back," Dorran said quietly. "I'm done." He looked at her. "I can make the arrangements for the tow."

She looked at him hopefully.

"You mean it's fixed?" she asked, producing a sudden hopeful smile.

Dorran's eyes narrowed.

"Obviously you weren't listening," he said.

Her face paled as she lifted her hand.

"No...wait—"

But Dorran shut the door. He didn't slam it in her face as the rage inside him demanded. Instead, he closed it slowly, conquering his dark impulses with the knowledge that he never had to see her again.

As the sirens sounded outside, Dorran ascended the stairs, holding his stomach with a grimace. He took a shower, dressed and sat in his comfortable black recliner. As he dug into his breakfast of boiled eggs, fruit, and milk, a sound reverberated on his door: three light taps.

"Come on in Max," Dorran called out.

The door opened and Max slowly entered the apartment. His face solemn, his eyes took on the look of focused anger.

"You okay?" the man asked.

"Have a seat," Dorran said, gesturing to the chair across from him. Max did so, filled his cheeks with air and blew them out.

"Skye admits to pulling the alarm, for which she didn't appear the least bit sorry. She actually sounded shocked that you quit on her car." He looked at Dorran. "Which, again, doesn't surprise me."

Dorran nodded slightly. "I don't need that."

Max nodded in agreement. "I know. I would have done the same. And for her prank, the police cited her a thousand-dollar ticket along with an invite to court."

Dorran snorted. "Real punishment there."

"So...you okay?" Max repeated.

Dorran nodded. "Yeah, just not the best wake up call."

"I'll talk with her dad today," Max said, getting up to leave.

"Sounds good. I'll be down later. I need to see Trey first."

Max swore under his breath and looked at the floor with a nod.

"I figured as much," he said, looking back up at Dorran. "All right. Later."

*

Dorran sat opposite Trey's army recruiter desk with its peeling gray paint. Trey held his cell in his hands, looking at some Facebook pictures.

"Yeah, this story already circulated. I see Skye standing in front of the shop talking to the police, but no pics of you. Take a look." He handed the phone to Dorran with a laugh. "You really blasted down the stairs buck naked?"

"Just about," Dorran replied.

Trey shook his head and laughed. "She's crazy. Reminds me of the time when a recruit accidently set fire in a mess tent. A lot of alarms went off, but they were the human kind." He looked up at Dorran. "Your waiver was officially approved today."

Dorran brightened. "Good."

"Okay. You ready for this?"

Dorran smiled. "Definitely."

"All right." Trey stood and Dorran copied his move. "Let's do this. Raise your right and repeat after me..."

Chapter 5
Fire

A thrill passed through Skye at the sight of Dorran's god-like body: buff, ripped, big guns. Choice words typically reserved for those in the enviable class of 'professional athlete'. Ignoring the panicked expression on his face, Skye was stunned at his physical display of beauty, something she'd never seen in any of her old boyfriends. Or anyone else for that matter.

"You set off the fire alarm?" Dorran yelled over the jarring noises.

Snapped back to the present, Skye put in her automated defense. "Well...yeah!" she retorted. "You think I was going to wait around until you ditch me with another excuse?" She stared him up and down again, not able to resist. "Though I have to say—you give quite a show," she added, hoping to lighten the moment.

"You like what you see?" he growled, plainly angry.

Skye shrugged, wondering if she had crossed some forbidden line. Had she misjudged him? Could he be unlike the jerks she knew, who always turned exhibitionist at the first opportunity?

"Maybe," she countered, not ready to back down. "But I was hoping for a car show more than a strip tease."

Dorran's expression morphed from surprise to irritation as he pointed his index finger in the air.

"Just a moment," he called out above the metallic clanging that chorused through the air. He closed the door and a few minutes later, the alarm died away.

But as the annoying sounds dwindled, a sense of dread welled. This was all wrong. Skye expected him to laugh off her prank. To strut his stuff. Do a stupid dance to humor her. It was all the more conspicuous by its absence.

Dorran acted different from anyone she had ever met. He had an air of—what was it? A healthy dose of self-respect? A sense of self control preventing him from chasing after anyone in a skirt?

He wasn't in the class of the rich, obviously. But here he was, the one in control of the situation—not her, despite the fact that he was the one who lacked clothes.

And Skye suddenly wanted to know why. What was it that made him this way?

The door slowly reopened and there he stood again, a god among men. But his eyes flashed at her, cold as ice.

"What's the matter?" she reacted with a glare, expecting Dorran to ream her over the coals for her juvenile prank. Would he start another volley of insults?

But his expression relaxed as if reconsidering. He spoke so softly she strained to hear him.

"Miss Larson, you can have your car back," he said, barely above a whisper. "I'm done." He looked into her eyes. "I can make the arrangements for the tow."

In a flash, Skye realized her miscalculation. She just lost the car, her summer freedom, and a chance to get to know Dorran. But she decided to play the dumb card, in hopes he might reconsider.

"You mean it's fixed?" She offered her best smile.

Dorran's eyes narrowed. "Obviously you weren't listening," he muttered, his disappointment plain.

Skye lifted her hand in a last act of desperation. Maybe he would forgive her stupidity, rethink his decision, give her another chance.

"No...wait!" she said.

But he was gone.

Sirens sounded a few blocks away as Max slowly drove up in his new red Jeep Gladiator and parked. His harried expression confirmed to Skye that her morning was just about to get worse.

*

As Skye hobbled back across the busy intersection to the Arrowroot Bakery construction site, she couldn't shake the numbness that permeated her entire being. Her car—the one thing she could really call her own—would be hauled away to some garbage heap and left to rust forever. And it was all her fault. Her temper had gotten the best of her. Again. And the one guy with an *amazing* body who she suddenly wanted to be with, was now out of her reach.

And for some reason Skye was still wrestling to understand, it hurt. Really hurt.

A fancy *Arrowroot Bakery Coming Soon* sign stood near pallets of wood, concrete and machinery. Skye greeted the workers and waited close to 40 minutes before her mom showed up, dressed in slacks and an apron, ready to start her day. But as Adelaide looked at Skye, her face tightened.

"Honey, what's wrong?" she asked, as Skye melted into her arms.

*

"Filet mignon and Caesar Salad is tonight's selection," Wallace announced with his shiny white smile. "With white chocolate, raspberry and almond trifle for dessert."

Skye watched her mother's reassuring smile from across the table as Charles nodded and complimented the butler. As much as she tried to mentally prepare for dinner, her heart blocked her every step of the way. Still feeling the sting from earlier, she knew it would be a miracle if the meal finished with her emotions intact.

Adelaide looked at her husband, her eyes taking him in, the adoration plain.

"How was your day, dear?" she asked.

"Quite busy," he replied, his eyes moving quickly between her and Skye. "Not the market, mind you, but rather more local matters." The man drew himself up as the salads were served, but he didn't speak until Wallace disappeared through the kitchen doors. And even then, it seemed as if

Charles struggled for the correct words. After a moment he sighed.

"First of all, I must say Skye that your behavior this morning was...disappointing." But the man eyed her with a look more resembling concern than anger. "That sort of activity can affect your future in more ways than you know." He paused, waiting for Skye's response.

"Yes, Father," she said, staring at the table in front of her, doing her penitent daughter part.

"Of course you are justified in being angry," the man continued. "The way this mechanic brushed you off was both unprofessional and rude."

Skye simply nodded.

"I spoke with the district attorney so you won't need to appear in court," he continued. "The fine will have to come from your monthly allowance, of course."

Another pause.

"Thank you, Father," she responded with a slight smile, though she felt no joy.

"And as for your car," the man said, and he paused.

She braced. Her BMW was to be towed off to some godforsaken place and she'd be given a new one, with all the family strings and restrictions attached. She felt her eyes begin to water but she fought it.

"I spoke with Max at length, and finally I was able to calm him down." The man chuckled. "He seemed more concerned about Dorran than the incident, which seemed rather odd. Mechanics aren't *that* hard to come by."

Skye sat ramrod straight. She forced her voice to emanate calm.

"Dorran quit?"

"Not today, no. But apparently he will be moving on soon," her father said. "Max suggested that the extra pressure Dorran is under to do this job is multiplied by your...presence. I think he is obsessing over nothing, really. And his claims about Dorran seem rather farfetched."

Skye looked to her mother, who nodded slightly.

"What claims?" Skye asked in a not-so-controlled voice. A twinge of dizziness hit her. Was she the reason why Dorran was going to leave?

Charles sat back in his seat. "One in a thousand can do the work he can," he said with a chuckle and a shake of his head. "Dorran is only a boy—perhaps skilled to some degree, but still inexperienced as a true craftsman. Max went on to claim that since Dorran came onboard, the shop has always more demand than they can handle. Losing him would cut his clientele in half." His brows furrowed. "So he says."

"What do we know about the boy, darling?" Adelaide asked sweetly. "His upbringing?"

Charles took a drink from his glass and set it down. "Nothing special. Just a commoner who moved from Denver when he turned 18. I think Finn Parker and his family played a part in that. The mother and father are not around. His younger sister lives with an aunt and uncle in Colorado."

Skye stared hard at the salad in front of her, processing the information. She'd never known anyone outside her social circle she'd give a second thought to. But Dorran Black didn't need social standing to get her attention. But now he seemed so unreachable and so desirable that she couldn't get him out of her mind. The image of his gorgeous body replayed itself like a constant headache.

"So, about your car," Charles said, looking straight at Skye. "We might be able to salvage the situation."

Skye brightened with a gasp. "How so?"

"If Max can convince Dorran to stay on the project—we would pay double the price. This way he would receive a large bonus for the work."

"That is wonderful news," Adelaide chimed in. "Isn't it, Skye?"

Skye nodded, her depression beginning to lift.

"Which would partly come from your allowance," Charles said. "But there is another matter." He paused and looked at Skye pointedly. "You must limit your visits to once a week, and only after the dust settles. Your presence in the shop seems to be... counterproductive, as Max put it." The man laughed again. "We should know by tomorrow if Dorran agrees." The man turned to his wife. "And how was your day, my dear?"

Adelaide lit up like a light bulb.

"Most of the interior has been renovated to some degree. I think it will be another week before we can start moving the new furnishings inside." She turned to Skye. "Our brilliant daughter has arranged an ad campaign through the local newspapers and television to be aired on opening day. She's pulled in talent from out of state who seem perfect for the job."

Charles Larson simply beamed at both of them as the filet mignon was served. But Skye missed it, her thoughts absorbed with her car and Dorran Black.

*

Skye lay back on her king-sized, four-poster bed with all its pink ruffles and lacing. She glanced around the huge bedroom that was assigned to her after she started college. This made number five since she was born in Coeur d'Alene General Hospital twenty years before. All the elaborate sofas and chairs and tables and murals and the chandelier and light wood flooring were all finished without any input from her.

And she hated everything about it.

She speed-dialed Sage, who picked up after one ring.

"Thought you forgot about me."

Skye snorted. "Just had dinner."

"Ahh, my condolences. So, what's the punishment? I mean, besides no more car."

"Since my presence is counterproductive, I can only meet once a week at the garage."

"Wait. You mean he's still gonna fix Caesar? I thought that was a dead deal."

"Father came to my rescue, as usual," Skye said, looking at the roof of her bed. The pinks reminded her of Pepto Bismol. "Said Max is gonna try to convince him to finish."

"Think he'll do it?"

Skye thought a moment before responding. "He was mad like my dad gets sometimes. Hard to say."

"So what did he look like? And I want more details than an Awesome Bod."

Skye felt her face burn, now wishing she hadn't called Sage a few hours earlier.

"I don't know," she replied. "Like Darrell I guess."

Sage snorted. *"Darrell? He's shaped more like a pug. Actually that's not fair to pugs. Darrell is more like a Porky Pug."*

Skye laughed, but didn't want to detail Dorran out loud in case she would lose the image in her head. "He was just really built—like he works out a lot," she lied.

"And in his underwear?" Sage asked. *"So like, he had a common bulge or uncommon?"*

Skye spluttered. "What's the difference?"

"Don't you remember sex-ed we took in high school?"

Skye felt her face burn again. "Yes, I remember." She paused, waiting for Sage to continue, but there was only silence. "Fine," she finally admitted. "It was uncommon."

Sage laughed through the phone. *"Jack pot! If you don't take him, I'm next in line!"*

"Cool your jets," Skye said. "I don't know if he's available. I've only met him three times, and then only where he works."

"And lives," Sage added with a giggle.

"So yeah. We'll just have to see."

"Ooh. A commoner. Does your dad know you like him?"

"Why should he know? That's none of his business." Another lie, Skye knew, but Sage was probing a bit too deep."

"Loving it!" Sage squealed. *"Secret romance! Cloak and dagger! Let me help?"*

"I might need an alibi," Skye said. "Some time."

"Oooooh pick me! Pick me!"

Chapter 6
Ice

Dorran wiped his brow as he lay on his Pro-Lift Creeper. Beneath a yellow Jaguar convertible, he wrestled with the side skirt rocker panel. Assured this special-order part would make for an easy replacement, he found that promise laughable. He had nothing but problems with something that should have taken him less than ten minutes to install. But the panel was over large by a fraction and refused to fit into place.

It was another hot Thursday afternoon, filled with demands on his every minute since he entered the shop. Half his projects were on hold because of faulty parts, missing parts, or back orders. The other half awaited his immediate attention. Max and Finn spent part of their morning explaining to customers why their cars were still unfinished. And this setback would simply add to that pile of incompletions.

Dorran closed his eyes, groaned aloud and was about to release a string of expletives when a soft voice interrupted his mental state.

"Mr. Black?"

He froze, wondering if he was hearing things. It sounded so quiet that it could be just the noise in his head. But he pulled the creeper forward anyway, only to see the last person he wanted to deal with on a stress-filled, scorching Thursday afternoon. Looking away, he swore under his breath but tried to put on his best smile under his grease covered face.

"Miss...Larson," he said, his voice monotone.

No longer in a boot, she wore a dark business attire, along with black high-heeled fancy shoes. He took one look at her and returned under the Jaguar, trying to reign in his temper. Skye Larson, the one who set off the fire alarm a week before, causing him to panic and run out of his house almost naked. Skye Larson, who had no regard for anyone's schedule except her own. A multi-millionaire's daughter who lived in a completely different universe and could never appreciate anything he did for her car.

With these thoughts rolling around in his head, he went back to work and pretended she was not there.

"Mr. Black," she said in a soft voice. "Could I please speak with you?"

The rage within cooled, as if ice water fell from the heavens and landed on his head. Was she actually being polite? It did not seem probable. His mind *had* to be playing tricks on him.

He rolled forward again, gave a heaving sigh, and this time sat up. Inwardly he tried to psyche himself up for a verbal assault he knew was coming.

"Yes, Miss Larson?" he said, mirroring her tone. "Would you like a car update?"

"It's Skye, actually," she said quietly, running her hands through her black Saint Laurent purse. She pulled out a thick envelope, took a few halting steps in his direction and offered it to him.

"What is it?" he asked, again mirroring her voice.

"Part of an apology," she said, looking him in the eye.

Dorran glanced over at Finn and Max, who stood stock still and stared at them. Finn's mouth was wide open.

Dorran looked back at Skye. "What part of an apology?" he asked. "Or is this a joke?" He knew the other shoe was just about to drop, and it would probably be a heavy one.

Skye's eyes narrowed but she held her composure, still leaning forward with the envelope. "No joke," she insisted. "Inside you'll find a check along with an invite to dinner at our house."

Dorran made no attempt to move. "I was told I'm receiving a bonus for this work," he said, feeling more confused than ever.

What do these people want from me? he wondered, irritation beginning to rise.

"Yes, but this is in addition to that."

Dorran looked around, trying to think of a proper response. She didn't insult him, but this offer seemed highly suspicious. As in, if it looks too good to be true, it probably is.

"No, thank you," he finally said with a slight shake of his head. He sank back down and returned to the underbelly of the Jaguar. But his head was at the right angle in which to watch her expression.

Skye Larson pulled back with a look of shock, which remained on her face for several moments. After the color returned to her face, she regained her composure and stuffed the envelope back inside her purse.

"Mr. Black, I do apologize for my rash actions last week," she said, staring at the ground in front of her. "I was angry when you refused to –"

As Dorran rolled the creeper out again, she stopped for a moment as if losing her train of thought. "When you drove away on your motorcycle," she continued. "I thought it would help you see my point." Her eyes did not meet his.

"And what point would that be?" Dorran asked. "That you can come here any time after hours and demand more of my time than I already have put into your car? Do you know how long I worked on your BMW?" His anger roared within.

Skye nodded as she looked over at Dorran's boss. "Yes, I do. Max told me everything." She turned to leave, but her right foot slipped and she fell halfway to the concrete before she righted herself. "I won't trouble you any further."

As she started to hobble away, a spasm of pain arced across her face. With hands on his hips, Max cleared his throat, glared at Dorran and gave Finn clear signals.

"Miss Larson!" Finn called as he ran to another part of the shop. "Just a second! Let me get you a chair!"

Max also motioned to Dorran, who nodded in understanding. In a flash he eyed Skye's right foot, swollen and red. With a rush of guilt, he stood, wiped his greasy hands as best as he could, took the chair from Finn and set it in front of Skye. He took a deep breath and looked at her.

"Please...sit," he said. And she did, looking at him expectantly.

"I need to change out of this," Dorran explained, pointing to his overalls. "And I will help you to your car."

Her eyes screamed at him for a brief second before cooling, as if she weighed something in her mind.

"All right," she said complacently.

Dorran raced up the stairs to his apartment, stripped off his greasy overalls and scrubbed his arms and face. After pulling on sweats and a t-shirt, he returned back to the shop.

Still sitting in the chair provided, Skye gave Dorran a humored smile.

"Did you want to see your car?" he asked, trying his best to be professional. "The trunk area is mostly complete and I'm waiting for the door covers to arrive."

"I saw it as I came in," Skye said, turning her head toward the back of the shop. "It's looking...good."

Dorran's eyes widened at the compliment, but they reverted before she seemed to notice. He offered his left arm which she gripped at once with both of hers. Dorran supported her as they slowly moved toward the parking lot, where a long black limo waited. But her right foot gave way with every step she took, until she stumbled almost to the ground.

"This isn't working," Dorran murmured. On sudden impulse, he gently picked her up, supporting both shoulder and legs. Skye sucked in her breath as Dorran carefully walked his way to the limo.

She weighed little more than a spare tire, though her grip on his shoulders felt like 120-foot pounds. Her aroma of cotton candy and lemon drops cleared Dorran's senses and filled him with some unknown energy.

A corpulent elderly man stood beside the black limo, holding Skye's door open, and gaping with wide eyes. His mannerisms and graying hair resembled a twitching overstuffed squirrel.

"Marcus, don't gape like a carp," Skye said mildly. "We're in public view."

"Yes ma'am, sorry ma'am," Marcus said stiffly as he looked away.

As if carrying a porcelain doll, Dorran set Skye slowly and gently inside the luxurious car. His eyes widened as he glanced at the sleek interior with its black leather seats, television screen and wet bar.

He knelt and ever so carefully unstrapped Skye's high heel before removing it from her right foot, now angry red and bruised. Skye took the shoe as he offered it.

"No pumps yet, Miss Larson," he said softly, looking into her slightly watery eyes.

She surveyed him intently for a few moments.

"You can call me Skye, Mr. Black." Her voice softened and her eyes pierced him.

Dorran gave a slight smile. "All right. Skye. You should keep your boot on. And you can call me Dorran."

"All right...Dorran." She watched as he withdrew and closed the door.

He nodded as the dazed driver waved and slowly drove away. Dorran could only stand there, trying to process what had just happened. Skye Larson, the multi-millionaire's daughter, just allowed him to carry her without so much as a single complaint. Or insult. And instead of trying to resist his intention to help, she clung to him as if it meant the difference between life and death.

He inhaled deeply, trying to recapture her perfume. Had she really smelled like cotton candy and lemon drops? He sniffed his own greasy arm with disgust.

But Dorran could not return inside the shop, not until he answered the question burning within. Did she like him? Was that possible? He remembered Skye's look, her calm demeanor, and most of all her apology. Was it just an act, or could she have been sincere?

But a wave of self-revulsion suddenly covered him, erasing any hope for a future with her. Dorran knew the odds, and his past could never measure up to hers. He was damaged goods. She was fine China.

But it's still fun to dream, he thought to himself.

He slowly returned to the shop, still wearing a partial smile. The clock on the wall announced it was closing time, but for some reason he didn't feel like leaving, like he suddenly possessed three more hours' worth of work energy.

As Dorran joined Max and Finn at the register, he noticed their faces giving something away. Neither would look at *him,* yet they eyed each other nervously.

"What's wrong?" he asked, eyebrows furrowed.

Max smiled slightly. "We typically don't carry our customers to their cars."

Dorran shrugged. "Part of our service to those in need."

Finn grinned. "Me thinks you be forming a soft spot for her."

Dorran's face burned as his internal defenses initialized. "She apologized. Unexpected, but it doesn't change anything."

"Plus an invite to dinner, and a check?" Finn pressed.

"Which he refused," Max added. "Interesting response."

"Sounds like *something's* changed," Finn said.

Dorran peered at his boss, defiant thoughts spinning in his head. "I don't belong with that crowd—never will," he retorted. "Why get my hopes up?"

"What's the harm?" Finn asked. "I'd go."

"You want to meet her father?" Dorran shot back. "Get tangled up in that? Be my guest."

Finn rubbed his jaw and nodded. "Point noted." He looked at Dorran. "Still, more money would be nice."

"More money which I'd owe for something else," Dorran said. "That's the way it works. You don't get something for nothing."

"Give her a chance, man!" Finn exclaimed. "You got nothing to lose. Be kind of nice to find out, wouldn't it?"

"And she did compliment you on the car's progress," Max noted. Dorran peered at the bearded man, whose expression became veiled. For a few seconds an uncomfortable silence hung in the air until finally Max turned and looked at the wall clock. "Well, let's call it. First round at Paddy's is on me."

*

Dorran flipped on the light switch to his spacious upstairs apartment—the second story over the shop. Everything was neat and organized, from the weight sets and punching bag on one side, to the simple furnishings of a black card table, brown couch and throw rugs on the other. Plants nestled along the three window stools that spread across the back wall. The light wood floor along with the off-white walls helped light up the apartment. A library of over a hundred books stood behind the couch against the wall.

"How come you're not socializing?" Finn asked as Dorran led the way inside. "And you hardly ate—one light beer and a salad?"

"Not that hungry," Dorran replied. "Just feel like working out."

"This place is set up," Finn said, eyeing the room. "You finally unpacked your books?"

"That was your mom," Dorran replied. "She said the place wasn't finished without a bookshelf." He paused. "Want to be my spotter?"

"Hang on," Finn said, making his way over to the card table. "This your newest project?"

A perfect paper replica of Howl's Moving Castle stood on one end, with its gaping mouth, huge red tongue, and all the colorful metal-like odds and ends that resembled a walking junkyard.

"Just finished," Dorran said, sliding onto his bench seat. He placed his hands to lift

190 pounds as Finn walked behind. "Late night project."

"I thought you were at 165?" Finn said, visibly impressed by the weights.

Dorran laughed. "It's been a while since we worked out," he replied before doing six reps.

"When do you find the time?" Finn asked, helping to lift the weight bar back onto the stand. "Or the energy?"

"Can't sleep sometimes."

A few moments went by and Finn changed the subject. "Hey, speaking of, my mom and dad keep bugging me about us getting together."

Dorran's face lit up. "Sure. Just let me know when. It's been a while."

Dorran lifted until his arms gave out. Finn took on the punching bag after sliding on some red and black gloves. Dorran held it as his friend nailed it with heavy punches.

"So, about Skye," Finn said, offering a slight smile.

Dorran sighed. "What about her?"

"I've heard stories."

Punch, went the bag.

"So? There's always stories about the rich and famous."

"She's not hanging around her old group as much this summer."

Punch. Punch.

"Hasn't hooked up with anyone yet, either," Finn continued.

Punch. Punch. Punch.

"Why do you think that is, Dorran?"

Dorran rolled his eyes. "You just don't give up," he complained.

Finn punched the bag again with his muscular arms, knocking Dorran around. He worked at it feverishly until sweat glimmered on his skin. Finally, he stopped.

"She's into you, man!" he said. "Add it up! Her smile. The money. And letting you carry her? Who does that?"

Dorran folded his arms. "Doesn't matter. My life—"

Finn interrupted with an exasperated sigh. "Isn't perfect," he said. "Yeah, since when is anybody's? You've been on your own for three years, Dorran! You got a lot going for you. Why do you keep short-selling yourself?"

"What if she finds out?"

"Of course she'll find out--sooner or later because her dad has all the connections. But there's more to you than that old life you left behind."

"She'll just take off," Dorran mused. "Just like the others. She'll be gone."

"How can you be so sure? What if she isn't like the others?" Finn persisted.

Dorran laughed. "You think that's possible?"

Finn paused. "Honestly, I don't know, but you can't spend your entire life hiding from what could be yours." He leaned against the bag. "Remember the Larson family isn't perfect, either. I did some digging to find out that the older sister, Liliane, had interesting issues."

"Liliane?"

"Skye's older sister by ten years. Went through a rebellious period, even checked into a psyche ward for a while. Eventually she left home. Cut ties with the family."

Dorran looked at his friend. "So what's your point?"

Finn folded his arms, the gloves still attached. He frowned.

"Can I say something?"

Those were loaded words. Finn asked this question only twice since they became friends. Once, when the police were watching his family. The other time was when he invited Dorran to live with his family after he left juvey. So whatever Finn was going to say would be something serious.

"Of course," Dorran replied evenly.

"Okay, so I've been watching you since you started this job and your new life. Three, no—four girls have showed interest but you shrugged them off. You are so tight inside and worried that someone will find out your past that it's like you're still living it. Like you're in your own self-made prison."

"What?" Dorran reacted. "I hardly ever think of juvey anymore."

"You don't ever talk to anyone but me about personal stuff," Finn retorted.

"That's because I can trust you."

"Yeah, I get that," Finn said. "But I'm not the only boy scout out there. What if Skye *is* the one for you?"

But fears of failure rode hard in Dorran's mind. He looked back at his parents constant bickering, their inability to be husband and wife, let alone loving and responsible parents. What if he turned out the same way? What if he ended up wrecking lives like that?

Finn took a step forward and looked him straight in the eye.

"Dorran," he said quietly. "Loosen up. I'm your best friend, and I hate to see you sell yourself short every time you step away from something that could be yours. You're not that kid in trouble anymore. He's gone. Forever. Dead. So let him go, okay? And all that attached crap. Start seeing yourself for who you are right now."

Dorran blinked a few times as he looked to the floor. He couldn't look Finn in the eye because his face burned. Like this was a bright light blazing on the degenerated, moldy skeletons of his closet. But at the same time Dorran realized Finn was in the wrong profession. He should have gone into psychiatry.

"Okay, doctor," he finally said. "I'll give it a try."

Finn brightened at once. "All right," he said cheerfully. "Hold that bag again for me, will ya?"

Chapter 7
Fire

Skye grabbed and bagged some chunks of ice from the limo bar before wrapping them around her swollen ankle. Although the shock of cold blanketed the pain, she didn't care. Her mind focused elsewhere.

Dorran Black. The handsome stud who wouldn't take a bribe. A principled hunk who rose above the mindset that money is everything and power is more. None of her old boyfriends would have hesitated to snatch up any offer from any member of her family, let alone grovel at her dad's feet during a dinner. And none of her exes would ever think of carrying her to the car.

A thought weighed on her mind. *Could* Dorran be the one for her? Could her Prince Charming be guised as a car mechanic?

"Miss Skye, should I bring you to the emergency room?" came the withered voice of her driver, Marcus.

Skye startled out of her thoughts and glanced at him. "No," she replied. "But I'll need someone to fetch my boot when we get home."

"Very good Miss," Marcus replied.

As the privacy panel began to close, she lifted her hand.

"Is there anything else, Miss Skye?" Marcus asked politely, as the panel paused.

She nodded. "Not one word of this to Wallace or my father."

"Miss?" The man looked confused.

"Dorran carrying me to the car."

"Of course, Miss," the old man replied with a slight smile. "It's nobody's concern but yours."

As the privacy panel closed, Skye's thoughts returned to Dorran's strong arms. He did not waver or hesitate in his steps, and he set her down gently and carefully onto the seat. When did anyone treat her like that? And his soft voice mesmerized her. His gentle words echoed again in her mind.

"*No shoes yet, Miss Larson.*"

His voice soothed her.

"*All right, Skye. You should keep your boot on. And you can call me Dorran.*"

Was a friendship blooming? Perhaps something more?

But the image of her father's face threatened what would be if she chose Dorran.

"*Just a commoner who moved from Denver...*" Those were his words, her father's typical description of anyone not in his social circle of the rich and powerful. An attitude that never seemed to bother her before, but now it blazed with hypocrisy. He thought Dorran was what? Inconsequential? Worthless? Insignificant? Most likely all those things, making Skye off-limits to him. But what her father didn't know...

*

Saturday morning Skye pushed a grocery cart through Wayfarer's Market, surveying its wide selection of health foods. Fourteen different types of gluten-free flours, including almond, buckwheat and tigernut, sat on one shelf alone. She wondered what each of these would look like on video if they were poured into a bowl and mixed.

As Skye placed a few bags of almond flour inside her cart, she eyed someone crossing a main aisle. The figure appeared as a blur, but a familiar one. Following, she found Dorran carrying a small green shopping basket, with veggies almost overflowing.

Skye hid from his direct line of sight, watching him shift the basket from one arm to the other. As a celery stalk fell to the floor, Dorran grabbed it and looked behind him, catching Skye's eye at the same time. She gave a friendly smile as his face turned crimson.

She casually made her way over as he hurriedly tried to organize his merchandise.

"Isn't it time to give the 'ol arms a break?" she asked. "Plenty of room in this cart."

Dorran eyed her few items as if briefly considering. He swung around in her direction.

"No thanks, I'm—"

The same celery as before sailed out, along with a bag of peppers, a bunch of bananas and a box of protein powder. Skye trounced on the runaways, scooping up the powder and bananas before he could think to protest. Into her cart they went, and she held out her hand.

"Give 'em over," she instructed.

Begrudgingly he handed the basket to her, at which point she placed his items all over her cart, and in no particular order.

"There!" she said cheerfully. "No more straining."

Dorran looked at his muscular arms with a wry smile. "You're versatile in that boot of yours," he said. As they continued down a spice aisle, he turned to her. "I thought your servants did the shopping."

"I'm not quite as helpless as that," Skye countered with a snort. "But this is for the Arrowroot Bakery. And it gives me ideas for advertising."

His eyebrows went up. "Advertising?"

She nodded playfully. "You know, things like television commercials, radio spots, magazine ads."

"I know what advertising is, Miss Larson."

She clucked her tongue and shook her head. "Call me Skye. You promised."

Dorran's face turned a shade darker as he looked away.

"I only meant I didn't get the connection between this food and a television commercial." His soft voice sounded like a mix of annoyance and intent.

Skye went into business mode.

"If the consumer is able to see the ingredients blend into the mixes and how they are prepared, they can almost taste the food as they watch my videos."

"Sounds delectable," Dorran admitted as he handled a bottle of meat seasoning. "Skye."

"It will be," Skye said. "By the way, the bakery opens early Monday."

"Is that so?" Dorran asked. "Perhaps I'll check it out."

"Would be ever so convenient for you, since it's right across your street."

Dorran nodded slightly. "I noticed that."

"But it is gluten free," she added. "Not necessarily to everyone's taste."

He put the seasoning away and looked at her.

"Actually, gluten free foods are my preference."

She threw him a deadpan look. "Are you saying that to impress me?"

With a single shake of his head, Dorran turned back to look at the spices. "Regular bread makes me sick for days." He shrugged. "So I stay away from it." He leaned in slightly. "How does that impress you?"

"A little," she replied. "But more if you were our first customer. Bright and early Monday." She offered her best dazzling smile.

"Do you deliver?" he asked, a twinkle in his eye. "We're awfully busy fixing other people's cars."

She considered a moment. "I'll think about it," she finally said. "For an outrageous charge of course."

"Of course," Dorran agreed. He looked down at her boot. "You shouldn't hobble across the street for nothing."

"I don't hobble," she said. "I limp."

Dorran laughed a little. "I don't know if there is a difference."

"There certainly is," she replied confidently. "A hobble is when someone walks weird, whereas a limp favors one leg. Want me to show you?"

Skye took a few steps forward in a dramatic wobbling demonstration. As she returned, she found Dorran lifting his hands as if in surrender. His head swiveled at the curious onlookers, some pausing to stare.

"Not necessary," he said, his face shading again. His eyes widened as if embarrassed by the attention they were getting. "I need to continue my shopping."

Not playful in public, Skye noted to herself. "All right," she said, eyeing the shopping cart. "What's next on your list?

You currently have broken celery, bruised bananas, protein powder, and milk."

"Health drinks, eggs, meat," Dorran replied. "And gluten free bread."

Skye gave an exaggerated bow and swept out her arm to the right. "Right this way."

Skye led Dorran around the store, pointing out other health foods he might like such as chamomile, peppermint, licorice, flaxseed, and papaya, courtesy of her research from the last two weeks. By the time they finished the shopping, the cart was almost overflowing, with Dorran's groceries stacked higher than Skye's. And after everything was bought and bagged, she noticed him suddenly tense.

"What's up?" she asked casually.

"I walked from home," he whispered. "I can't carry all of this." His face was redder than ever, his teeth grit in apparent exasperation.

"Well...hire an Uber or take a taxi," Skye said. As he processed the information with a quick nod, she continued. "Better yet, I'll give you a ride." But her face prickled at the double meaning. "There's plenty of room in the limo. It's not a problem."

Dorran looked into her eyes. "I don't want to impose."

Skye shook her head, her heart speeding up. "It would be my pleasure."

His eyebrows shot up and a slight smile appeared. "Your...pleasure?"

Her face prickled again. "Kind of lonely sitting all by myself with all that room." She shrugged. "Just me and the driver. Besides, how would it look if I just abandoned you on the street with four big bags of groceries? Hardly what I would call being a..." She trailed off and looked away, this time feeling her own face burn.

"Friend?" Dorran finished for her.

Skye smiled. "Let's just say a rescuer. I rescue shoppers who don't know when to quit."

Dorran swept all of his and her grocery bags into the cart.

"All right, I accept your generous offer," he said simply. "Besides, it's impolite to watch you hobble out to your car with all this food."

"Limp," Skye corrected. "But yes," she continued, putting her arm inside his. "It can be a pain."

"What about your driver, Marcus?" Dorran asked as they made their way outside. "Isn't he supposed to help?"

"Of course."

"I don't see him anywhere," Dorran said, his eyes scanning the parking lot.

Skye bit her lip, wondering for a brief moment how much she should explain. "Marcus and I have an agreement," she said. "He doesn't tattle where I go and I simply text him when I'm ready. In turn, he drives wherever he wants and I don't say a thing."

Three seconds later the black limo pulled up in front of them and its trunk popped open. Dorran put the bags in the back as Skye slid into her seat and waited, hoping he would sit by her.

As Dorran climbed inside, his eyes widened.

"Spacious," he said.

"They usually are," she replied as he slid next to her.

"Good morning Dorran," Marcus greeted. "And welcome aboard."

Dorran nodded his thanks as the privacy panel closed and the limo slowly moved out of the parking lot.

Skye swept her hand toward the bar, with its selections of fine wines and beers.

"Care for a drink?" she asked. "There is a large assortment." She wondered if he drank at all, given his apparent healthy lifestyle.

Dorran smiled and shook his head slightly. "A bit too early for me, thanks." He leaned forward in his seat, looking uncomfortable. Did she offend him by offering alcohol? Would he change his mind and ask to get out?

"Do you water ski?" Skye asked, out of desperation to break the uncomfortable silence.

Dorran gave a blank expression. "Water ski?"

"Yes," she said. "You see, you take a boat out and—"

Dorran laughed. "I understand what water skiing is...Skye," he said, his eyes looking deep into hers. "I've been on the lake a few times."

Skye's heart skipped a beat. "Good to know," she replied. "Because you're invited. Next Saturday at Fern Lake. One o'clock at the boat landing. I have all the gear so you don't need to bring anything."

Dorran brightened with a nod. "Sounds like a fun way to spend 4th of July. But I was wondering," he added.

"What?" she asked, swallowing. She wondered if he was going to give an excuse and back out.

"Do you give every rescued shopper a limo ride and a lake invite?"

Skye tilted her head. "You're actually the first," she admitted. "A test case."

"I take pleasure in being your test subject," Dorran said, finally relaxing back into the seat. A few seconds later he pointed to the outside. "Here we are. My place."

Skye wished the ride would have been longer, or that Marcus got lost somewhere, but no.

"I can help you with the groceries," Skye offered.

"I got this," Dorran said as he climbed out of the car, but not before he glanced at her boot once more. "But thanks for the offer." He turned with a wink and, she thought, a slight look of longing. "See you later, Skye Larson."

"Dorran," she replied with a slight nod.

And then he was gone, leaving her alone and feeling more empty than ever.

Chapter 8

Ice

Dorran reclined on his brown couch, staring at the boot camp info and official letter that came from Trey Hunter. He was to report to Fort Jackson, South Carolina, on August 2nd. He would fly out from Boise August 1st, at 4 p.m.

A sense of gratitude welled. He would finally launch out and make something of himself in the Big Wide World. Earn a degree with the Army, and later run his own auto business. Eventually settle down and raise a family. Someday.

Immediately, Skye Larson's face came to mind. But Dorran knew better than to entertain any romantic notions. Given his background that relationship would never—could never—go anywhere. It was better to enjoy her company as a friend and nothing more. Thoughts of them together were pure fantasy and end up being a disappointment, so he wiped them from his mind.

He still felt some guilt about leaving Max and Finn, however, but this *was* his time. If he didn't leave now, he never would. He looked around at the apartment, with everything in its place, tidy and clean. But he couldn't imagine living here much longer. Granted it was nice, and he appreciated the free rent, which allowed him to save a nice chunk of money. But it still tied him to the shop, with nowhere else to go.

He refocused. August 1. He'd tell Max and Finn on Monday. That gave him 26 days to wrap up his projects, pack his stuff, get into shape and be shipped off to his new adventure. He could hardly wait.

*

As Dorran lifted the shop bay door Monday morning, he found Skye standing outside, holding a stack of boxes covered with Arrowroot Bakery insignia. Her flushed face held a look of impatience mixed with a steady, business-like smile.

Dorran's eye widened. "Skye!" he said happily. "Let me get those!" As he took the boxes from her arms, she picked up her purse, along with a thick, long envelope, and limped behind him.

"Compliments of my mother," she said. "She wouldn't let me charge you for them."

"And why is that?" Dorran asked as he led her into the office, and set the stack on the cluttered counter. He shoved the invoices, shop manuals and small boxes aside.

"Promotional advertising," Skye said with folded arms. "For you and your customers."

Dorran took the top box from the stack and opened the lid, to find a dozen fresh chocolate cupcakes.

"Wow. Thanks!"

"There's more," she said business-like, opening the over-sized envelope. "Some posters for you to hang."

"Of course, I'm sure Max will love it."

Dorran scanned the beautiful 18 x 24 advertisement that provided the store's days and hours of operation. The backdrop of chocolate batter falling into a bowl looked so real, Dorran was tempted to lick it.

Skye stifled a tired yawn. The slight bags under her eyes made it clear she'd been up a while.

"How's the beast?" she asked as she looked longingly at her half-finished BMW M3.

Dorran leaned against the counter. "Door work almost complete."

"Can't wait until I regain my freedom," she said with another yawn. "My morning started at four."

Dorran pulled out the orders sheet for her and studied it a moment.

"Still waiting for the side skirt, headlights, front bumper and hood to arrive. Most of it should be here this week."

Skye's mouth fell open. "So you mean..."

Dorran gave a slight smile. "With any luck you'll have it back by next Tuesday."

Skye squealed and gave Dorran a happy hug before he realized what happened. Her embrace threw him off—both mentally and physically.

"Thank you," she breathed happily. "This means—you can't imagine how much this means." She beamed with giddiness and looked into his eyes. "See you Saturday."

Her stare almost unnerved him as did her hug. "Wouldn't miss it," he reassured her, before his brain switched back on. "Wait. Let me walk you back. Shop doesn't open for another ten minutes."

"And I'm here in any case," Finn called out as he entered the shop. His handsome face suddenly lit up. "Do I smell doughnuts?"

Dorran let Skye lean in close as they crossed the busy Auto Park Road intersection. The street seemed overly busy for this time of day, and Dorran soon realized why. The Arrowroot Bakery was full of customers with no available parking spaces.

"We opened at five with a line waiting outside," Skye said, with a hint of tiredness.

"Good start to your business," Dorran said. "You must have a knack for advertising."

Skye looked over at him with a satisfied expression. "I do have my moments," she said. She pointed. "And this just happens to be one of them."

Skye gave Dorran a tour of the busy bakery, showing off the glass casings, inset shelves along the back walls, jars filled with candies, racks of cupcakes, ceiling lights highlighting the menus on the back walls, and much more. The place was thick with hungry customers, some who braved the store with small children, who pointed at the bright colored candy jars. Others dressed in business suits, waiting for their morning coffee.

The smell of donuts and coffee overwhelmed Dorran's senses and his stomach growled twice.

"Want a coffee?" Skye offered. "I'm buying."

"My treat," Dorran countered. "Pick whatever you want," he said as he joined one of four long lines.

Dorran ordered a scone and Mocha Moonrise for himself and a berry muffin and Mocha Raspberry for Skye. Mrs. Larson, acting as hostess, guided Skye to a tiny table in a far corner of the bakery. The woman wore a large apron speckled with flour, her hairdo had gone partly awry, and she could not have looked any happier. But when she saw Dorran for the first time, her face paled as if she saw a ghost.

"Mom, this is Dorran," Skye introduced.

"Oh my!" she said with a crooked smile and nervous laugh. "How you do look like Darrell!" After composing herself she wiped her hands on her apron and offered her hand. "Pleased to meet you, Dorran. Skye has told me so much about you."

Dorran looked at Skye. "She has?"

"Oh yes, about how you are taking such good care of her car." She looked around the room. "What do you think of our little bakery?"

"It is very nice," Dorran smiled. "And thank you for sending us the treats, Mrs. Larson."

She put up her hands in a flutter as her face colored. "Oh, please. That was my mother." She added a small laugh. "Call me Adelaide."

"Adelaide," Dorran repeated. "Nice to meet you."

Skye's mother looked around the crowded store. "Well, lots more customers to help," she said cheerfully. "If you'll excuse me." She looked at Skye. "See you in a bit?"

Skye nodded.

After they sat down and started eating, Dorran broke the silence.

"Your mom is...nice, after a fashion."

Skye looked at him strangely. "Something you weren't expecting?"

"Completely unexpected."

Skye laughed. "Why is that?"

He took a deep breath and met her gaze. "Let's just say that the wealthy people I've encountered are usually best avoided."

"Does that include me?"

"Are you wealthy, Skye Larson?"

"No, but my parents are."

"Then you're probably safe to be around. For now."

She snorted. "Thanks. But maybe you haven't hung around the *right wealthy people*."

"Possibly," he admitted, still staring after her mom. She bounced from one customer to the other, greeting them cordially. "Is it an act with her, or is she really that friendly?" he asked without thinking.

"When Mom is free to be herself, that's what you get," Skye said quietly. "Away from...everything and everyone else."

"You don't see this often?"

As if caught saying something wrong, she flushed and stammered. "Well, you know, you have to be careful."

"I get it," Dorran said quietly. "Keeping up appearances and all that. It can't be easy."

Skye leaned forward. "Why are you being so judgmental toward my family?" Her eyes narrowed. "What did they ever do to you?"

"Nothing," Dorran said with a straight face. "I also find it safer to be careful."

"In your case, you mean run away."

Dorran tilted his head. "Not worth the risk," he replied. "Years back I got burned by some rich guy my dad and I worked for. I've been paying for it ever since."

"What kind of work?" Skye asked, looking at him intently.

"Ah," Dorran replied, not expecting the question. He felt his face heat up with embarrassment, but he had no reason to lie. "It wasn't legal. My point is we trusted him, but he had no qualms about walking away when trouble came."

"Sounds like an interesting past," Skye said.

Dorran felt his face tighten. "And one to which I will never return." He pulled out his cell phone to check the time. "And speaking of...I better get to work." He stood and gave her a genuine smile. "Thanks for the tour."

"Of course," she replied. But this time she didn't smile back.

Chapter 9

Fire

Skye leaned back on the light brown Burrow Nomad Sofa and peered at the vaulted ceiling with the attractive dark brown wood beams. Her face relaxed a bit.

"So, Miss Larson, are we going to talk today or spend another hour in horrific silence?"

That came from her counselor, a severe looking British woman with a business outfit to go with it. She had listened to Adelaide Larson for years, but for the past few months Skye mostly acted like a mime with attitude.

"Talk."

The elderly woman's face softened, momentarily erasing a number of deep wrinkles beneath her eyes. But her eyebrows shot up, multiplying the creases to her forehead. "Whatever initiated the change?" she asked in a tone dripping with sarcasm.

"Just have a lot on my mind. But first things first. This conversation is confidential."

"As always," came the counselor's clipped reply.

"Not for anyone's ears."

"Yes, that's the general idea."

"Not even my mother's."

The counselor paused and sucked in a breath. "Of course."

"Swear it, Marjorie."

Marjorie's face looked stunned.

"Swear it," Skye continued. "Or I'll never darken these doors again."

"Goodness. A bit dramatic, don't you think?"

"Not really, since my father's house employees routinely betray my confidences."

"All right, fine," she said. "Your words will never go outside these walls."

"So, what should we talk about?" Skye asked.

Marjorie threw up her hands and sighed. "A few things do come to mind! How is your recovery? Your thoughts about Darrell? Life without a car? How was university this year? Have you heard from your sister?"

Skye gave her a smug smile as she reclined further on the couch.

"Yes."

Marjorie glared and folded her arms. "Yes to what, exactly?"

"Liliane and I are on speaking terms."

A look of shock covered the elder's face.

"Really?" Her eyes shifted around the room, obvious calculations apparently working in her brain. "How so?"

"I call her up and talk. She does the same."

"Skye, this is beyond madness," she complained. "Details please."

"Actually, I'm coming to appreciate how brave and strong my sister was when she left. My parents put her through a lot."

A few moments of empty silence passed between them, making Skye wonder if Marjorie had heard her words.

"And you are starting to go through the same...challenges?"

"Starting? Hardly. It's been my life for the last five years, but I hide it better than Liliane. She always spoke her mind, much to my parent's increased stress levels."

Marjorie uncrossed her arms. "So, how is Liliane?"

"From our May conversation, it sounds like she's doing quite well, despite everything. She has an apartment in Seattle and works as an environmental engineer. And she's made some really close friends."

The counselor sat back, in obvious reflection. She removed her reading glasses and rubbed them with a cloth. Skye could have sworn her eyes watered for a few seconds.

"That is good," she answered in dull tones. "Glad you are talking with her." She peered out the huge glass window overlooking a grove of trees. "So, what else is going on?"

Skye's back wriggled slightly. "You mean, besides how I hate school, how Darrell is a sex pervert, or how my freedom this summer is totally stripped away?"

"Your choice, though I heard that Darrell is still in hospital and things aren't looking good for him. You still want to press charges?"

"How did you know about that? I never said anything."

"You never said anything in any of our earlier sessions, but that's not really the point, is it?"

Skye glared and said nothing until Marjorie gave in.

"All right, your mother wanted me to prompt you into saying something during our glorious time together. That was one of her *open-Skye up* suggestions."

"Darrell is beyond history," Skye blurted out, reacting more than thinking. "He's an immature, hormonal-driven, twit." She envisioned Dorran, suddenly realizing the huge contrast between the two. Dorran had it all and didn't go around bragging about it. She couldn't recall anything redeemable about Darrell except her dad's recommendation.

The counselor's face twisted.

"What?" Skye asked, wondering what she said that was so wrong. In any event it was the truth.

"Whatever your feelings for that young man, you might want to know that Darrell's condition has worsened. It doesn't appear like he has much time left."

Skye narrowed her eyes. "What?"

"It's no secret, so I'm not betraying any confidences, if that's what you're wondering," the woman said defensively.

"No," Skye replied, her voice faltering. She swallowed. "I just hadn't heard." Guilt crept in as she recounted that fateful date with Darrell. Would his death be on her hands? To add that on top of everything else gone wrong, would certainly take years to get over.

"Do you want to talk about what happened?"

Skye shook her head. "I gave my statement to the police and that was hard enough. Didn't you see it on the news?"

"Well, yes, but all I understood was that he wasn't wearing his seat belt when another car forced you off the road. Beyond that is mere speculation."

"Let's talk about something else."

"All right." Marjorie raised a finger. "Last up, we have your stripped-away freedom."

Skye sighed happily. "Not for long."

"Not for long? What do you mean?"

"Dorran said my car will be ready sometime next week." A true smile came over her face at the thought of his hands working on it, making it perfect again.

"And who is Dorran?"

"The mechanic."

Marjorie cleared her throat. "I saw pictures of the BMW. Do you seriously think anyone can put it back together?"

Skye nodded, her smile returning. "If anyone can, it would be him."

"I see," Marjorie said, her mouth slowly forming a crooked smile. "Is romance in the air?"

Skye wondered at that question. Dorran's attitude about rich people was plain. Could she ever convince him otherwise, or was it a lost cause?

Chapter 10
Ice

Dorran's bike rumbled as it geared down and slowly entered the crowded Fern Lake parking lot. Heads swiveled his way as Dorran scanned for Skye and her boat. He didn't like unwanted attention, but he knew there was something about a growling '69 Honda CB750 that couldn't be ignored.

Skye waved at him while leaning against a Chevy Silverado, hitched to a MasterCraft Prostar. Dorran's mouth almost unhinged at the negligible clothing she wore, revealing numerous curves and lines previously unseen.

As he powered down his bike and parked beside the boat, he noticed she wasn't alone. Two others in skimpy bikinis waited nearby. Dorran recognized Sage, the twenty-something gorgeous friend of Skye, who met him at the shop in June. He remembered how she tried to keep Skye civil.

"I thought I was early," Dorran said apologetically, trying unsuccessfully to refocus away from the bikinis.

Skimpy swimwear does strange things to guys' perceptions, and all three looked more like Miss America beauty contestants instead of college students. But their scant clothing revealed far more than one would ever see on television. Dorran felt glad for the dark sunglasses that hid his wide, popping eyes.

"You're early," Skye replied. "But this place fills up fast on Saturdays and we wanted to reserve a spot." She turned to her friends. "You remember Sage."

Dorran gave a slight nod as she looked him over head to toe.

"And this is Olivia," Skye continued, gesturing to a brunette with the face and body of a goddess. In fact, all of them could claim they came from Mount Olympias and Dorran would have believed them.

So much flesh in so little space, he thought.

Olivia placed her hand on Dorran's left shoulder, sending a tingling sensation shooting through him.

"Nice to meet you, finally," she said in a sweet voice, while looking him up one side and down the other. "You've got the face of Darrell and the body of...well, definitely someone else. Don't you think you'll be too hot in all those clothes?"

Dorran glanced down at his white-water sports shirt and knee-length black swim trunks, glad his shorts held extra airspace, since his manhood threatened to inflate. His face heated up as he tried to think of a response.

"He's definitely not anything like Darrell," Skye interrupted. "And he's my date, Olivia. Your man stayed home, remember?"

Olivia's white teeth sparkled as she slowly shook her head. "Mm-mmm. I don't know where my man is," she said. "But when I look at *him*, I don't even know if I have a man."

Skye and Sage laughed while Dorran's face burned hotter.

"I sure don't," Sage murmured. "But I'm currently in the market." She gave Dorran an expectant smile.

Skye cleared her throat, giving Sage and Olivia the happy/evil eye. "Let's get this beast launched before you two embarrass yourselves."

"Too late," Olivia said softly. "But around him, I don't mind."

Skye took Dorran's hand and faced her friends. "You two ride in the back. This one will be safer with me."

Sage and Olivia hopped into the truck bed, happy faces turning disappointed. As Skye slowly drove the truck and trailer to the ramp, Dorran let out a sigh.

"Your friends are...welcoming," he said.

Skye laughed. "Thanks. I don't think they know what to do with you."

Dorran looked at Skye. "You mean eat me or make me their pet?"

Skye nodded. "To Sage and Olivia, you're an unknown," she said. "Like you are to me."

Dorran's eyes narrowed while he tried to understand.

"Meaning?"

"I've never seen you with anyone else."

"I don't have a girlfriend if that's what you mean."

"So that makes you open season, at least for Sage and Olivia."

Dorran relaxed a bit and decided to go along with the game.

"But not you?"

Skye's smile disappeared. "I thought I wasn't worth the risk. And I don't chase boys."

But Dorran didn't back down. "Like I also said," he replied, his voice cautious and slow. "My experience has taught me to be careful."

The truck stopped as Skye turned the wheel. She looked at Dorran.

"Some say those who are too careful eventually find themselves alone." She sighed and looked at the dash. "I can't believe it. I'm sounding like my mom."

At least you have one, Dorran thought. But he pondered Skye's words, having been alone since he was fifteen. But his loneliness helped protect him from abusive relationships, of which he'd already had enough.

"I've got..." he began, but he couldn't finish. Should he tell her about signing up with the military?

"Big plans?" she said softly. "Where are you going, Dorran Black? And more importantly, who are you taking with you?"

Dorran felt dazed. Did she just invite him into her life? Was this promising to be a lot more than just friendship? But at the same time, it seemed like she just stared into his soul and saw every fear, uncertainty and insecurity he tried to hide.

He couldn't stop his face from tightening before Skye saw it and turned away.

"Sorry," she said with a sheepish smile. "It's really not my business." She motioned with her hand. "Can you help guide the boat back?"

"Sure," he replied, hopping out of the truck. He expertly led the trailer back, but her words unnerved him. Was he really an unknown to her, or did she see him for who he really was? Was his thick mask finally melting away?

The feelings of exposure that filled him were reminiscent of his vulnerable childhood. Dorran knew exploitation was right around the corner, and these three Olympian goddesses could dish it out like experts. Should he have declined the lake invite? It wasn't too late to leave if he could think of a plausible excuse. But nothing came to mind.

Yet something inside hoped it could be different from what his fears predicted. Perhaps Skye would eventually understand him and be a friend like Finn. Someday. But that takes time and trust, both of which he didn't have. And by August he'd be gone. Forever.

So he managed to push his thoughts away, reform his mask with a smile, and guide the boat back perfectly into the water.

*

"You're up first."

Olivia's hand ran up and down Dorran's left side while Sage caressed his right shoulder and eyed his muscular chest.

"I'd say medium." Sage opened a small closet and pulled out a life vest. "Skye drives until she skis."

"We handle the guests," Olivia added. "So you're all ours."

It was all Dorran could do to focus on the life jacket and not ogle at the immense beauty pressing in on all sides. His heart sped up as Skye entered the cockpit and bent low to open a cooler—right in front of him. She left nothing to the imagination.

"Ready?" she asked, pulling out a red Gatorade and handing it to him.

"I might need a refresher," Dorran said meekly, suddenly wanting Skye a whole lot nearer.

"We can arrange that," she replied. "Dry dock or water?"

"Water," he replied, staring at the floor.

"What's wrong, Dorran?" Olivia teased. "Don't like what you see?"

"Or are we too much for you?" Sage asked, moving in closer.

"By the look of things, I think he's getting overwhelmed," Skye said with a smile.

Dorran instantly covered the front of his trunks with his hands, his face lighting up again. Was this turning into a party?

"Do you think I'm pretty?" Olivia said, sliding her hand down his back.

"Or me?" Sage asked, gently caressing his chest.

Skye stood in front of him, arms folding, with an expression of, "And how do I rank?"

Dorran choked. "You all look...great," he said.

"But who do you consider beautiful?" Skye pressed, closing in so he could feel her warmth, even on this hot July day.

Dorran's mind reeled, desperately searching for the right words. Suddenly a phrase popped into his head, something he recently read.

"Every woman is beautiful," he said. "It just takes the right man to see it."

Olivia and Sage sighed happily as they giggled and melted away to other parts of the boat. Skye's smile widened as her eyes met his.

"And you sir, you're very attractive," she replied. "Therefore, I will stare at you." She came forward, took his face in her hands and kissed his cheek. "Congrats, you passed."

"I almost *passed* out," Dorran admitted.

"With flying colors," she continued, taking a step back. "Call it an initiation, but we like to filter out the pervs and psychos before we get out on the water."

Dorran took a relieved breath and wiped his forehead. "Makes sense."

"Call it our insurance policy, but we had to make sure." She turned to leave. "Be back in a minute. I'm going to change."

"Change?" Would she change out of her current skimpy swim suit?

"Into something more *comfortable*."

He stared at her, his heart sinking a little. He had grown very fond of her appearance in the last five minutes. But soon Skye, Sage and Olivia returned, dressed in more modest swimwear, more suitable for a Miss America Pageant.

Ten minutes later Skye was with him in the water, giving instruction.

She touched his right knee.

"Pull your knees to your chest, with your arms around them and the rope between the skis."

119

"Check."

"Let the life-jacket keep you on top of the water and lean back."

He did so.

"Bring the rope in between the tips of your skis with the handle between your body and the ski tips."

"Okay."

She placed her hand on his chest.

"Keep your skis pointing straight forward, close together with the tips. While leaning back with your knees to your chest, bring your ski tips up out of the water, keeping your skis straight and close together. They should be no more than hip width apart."

"You sound like a competent teacher."

"I've had practice," Skye replied with a straight face as she touched his right arm. "Keep your arms straight so the boat pulls you out of the water and up on your skis. If you try to bend your arms or pull yourself up out of the water, you'll lose your balance and fall."

"Got it."

"The skis should be directly underneath you even though you are leaning back slightly. Do not stand up immediately. Keep your eyes directly ahead. That's it. Good luck!"

"Thanks."

Skye's eyes narrowed. "Did I just waste my time on a pro?"

Dorran shrugged. "Never hurts to have a refresher."

*

After Dorran's fifth failure at attempting to launch, Skye jumped in the water and joined him.

"Sorry," Dorran said quickly. "Guess I'm not as good as I thought. Maybe I need another lesson."

"With what part, exactly?" Skye asked, her eyes amused.

"With being alone."

Skye cocked her head and signaled to her friends.

"I'll need my gear!" she called out.

A few minutes later both Dorran and Skye skied on the water effortlessly, with Sage driving and Olivia watching.

Dorran found himself grinning like the Cheshire cat. Mission accomplished.

"Fast learner!" Skye called out from the other side of the wake.

"A flat-out miracle!" Dorran shouted back. "You're an amazing teacher!"

"But am I curing your loneliness?" Skye asked, just barely loud enough for Dorran to hear.

"Beginning to!" he answered back.

Chapter 11
Fire

Skye's mind was in a daze but she kept looking forward, trying to pretend everything was okay, or would be okay eventually. She stood at a crosswalk holding two boxes of doughnuts and other pastries, courtesy of Arrowroot Bakery. She eyed Max's Auto Body Shop just a few hundred yards away, on the other side of the street, and sighed. This should have been the best day of the summer for her. She was on her way to pick up Caesar, her newly fixed red BMW. But so far, it was one of the worst.

As Skye stepped forward into the street, two sets of arms grabbed her and pulled her back. Her boxes went flying, but a girl in her early teens managed to catch them before they exploded on the ground.

Half a second later, a black sportscar raced by where Skye would have been. Shaking with fright, she looked at her rescuers. A man and his teenage son, still holding her arms, and looking at her in alarm.

"Thanks!" she breathed. "Not paying much attention this morning."

"Are you alright?" the man asked, slowly letting go of her sleeve.

"Thanks to you," Skye replied, taking back the boxes from the girl.

The signal changed and Skye quickly crossed after looking both ways. She felt her flushed face begin to cool as her adrenaline levels subsided.

"They need to reduce the speed on this street," Skye heard the man tell his son. "Before there's a tragedy."

*

By the time Skye reached Max's Auto Body Shop, its doors were open, ready for business. She took several long, deep breaths before walking inside. Dorran was at work, fixing the tailgate of a gorgeous Lemon Ice pearl 1953 international. The truck looked like it just came off the factory floor.

"Skye, what's wrong?" came Dorran's concerned voice. In seconds he was by her side, his face anxious. He took the boxes from her and stood, blocking her path.

Skye suddenly realized her arms shook uncontrollably and she crossed them. Her legs felt wobbly as well and she leaned to one side.

"Bad morning," she said through a forced smile.

"What. Happened?" Dorran demanded, putting the boxes down, pulling a chair over and setting her gently in it. "Talk to me."

Skye swallowed, feeling ridiculous. "I stepped onto a crosswalk before the signal turned. Almost got creamed by a sportscar."

Dorran's face turned dark. "Everyone drives too fast on that street."

Skye laughed. "That's what my rescuers said."

"But you're okay."

"I'm fine." She stared at him a few seconds before turning away. "So, the car is finished?"

Dorran slowly held up his hand. "Wait. You're not the type to blunder into traffic without thinking. Did something else happen?"

Can he read my mind? Skye wondered. She felt her eyes moisten but stopped it with sheer will. She returned Dorran's intense gaze.

"My car?" she repeated.

Dorran's face softened and he offered his hand. "This way."

He led her to the parking lot in back, just below the rear apartment window, and to the shiny, red, 2018 BMW M3, now perfectly restored.

Skye gasped. "This is my car? It looks brand new!"

"Probably better!" Max said, emerging from the shop with a great big smile. "And it's all yours. Paperwork is all taken care of." He handed her the keys and she hopped inside. Dorran opened the passenger door and joined her.

"Thanks," she said. For a while a genuine smile crossed her face. There were no scratches or dents, all the normal wear and tear was completely washed away. Everything even smelled brand new. But as her thoughts reminded her of the morning's shocking news, her smile turned forced.

Max excused himself with a "Thanks for the goodies," along with a *see you later* and a wave, but Dorran stared at her intently.

"Something else is wrong," he guessed. "What's going on?"

"It really is nothing for you to worry about," she said, trying to be stronger than she knew she was. Her eyes brimmed with tears. Again.

Dorran took her hand, his eyes more intense than ever. "Skye, tell me. Please."

She took a breath, dreading telling it to someone else, because it would make it real as day. Up to that point it could stay inside her mind, perhaps even remain only a fantasy. But it had to come out. She couldn't hold it in any longer.

She took in a deep breath. "Darrell—my ex-boyfriend, died last night." She stared at the floor, unable to meet Dorran's eyes.

"What? How?"

"Brain hemorrhage," she said, barely above a whisper. "At first, they thought he would recover. But his injuries were too severe."

Dorran placed his hand on hers.

"It wasn't your fault," he said plainly.

"I know," she replied. "But I was the driver."

"If he had worn a seat belt—" Dorran said.

"I know," she snapped, having heard that a million times before. She sighed. "The funeral is Saturday and Father wants me to give a speech."

"You're kidding. Your dad told you to eulogize your ex-boyfriend?"

Skye nodded, her stomach lurching. "Our families are close so...it's expected."

"You mean business close?"

She nodded again. "Dad has serious business connections all over Idaho. Sometimes I think I'm one of his charity dolls."

"Charity dolls?"

Skye laughed. "Something he loans out to dads needing a girl for their sons. Darrell was number four."

"Wait. All your previous boyfriends came from business relationships?" Dorran asked, eyebrows raised.

"Yep, the only ones he'd allow. And before you ask how I would ever consent to that, you have to understand my family."

Uncomfortable silence filled the car as Skye thought about facing all those people at the funeral who would blame her for Darrell's death. They didn't have all the facts, but even if they had, it would make no difference in their judgmental minds. She would take the blame.

"So," Dorran said with a smile. "You want to go for a test drive? I mean, we don't want any problems to crop up unawares."

"Unawares?" Skye found herself asking. "Who says that, anyway?"

But Dorran simply smiled and made no reply.

The engine purred to life as Skye remembered the last time she was in this car. *At least Dorran is buckled in*, she thought, *and he won't do anything stupid*. Or at least she hoped.

She made her way downtown to Calypsos Coffee, one of her favorite coffee shops, where anyone dressed in muddy work clothes to fancy suits was welcome. A few tables were filled, but morning rush was mostly over and they were seated far from any other table. Skye felt grateful for the privacy, knowing that no one from her dad's business would dare come here to spy on them.

It was time to ask him. She needed someone like Dorran in her life, today more than ever. But doubt held her back, fear gnawed inside at the answer she didn't want to hear. Would he reject her because of her family? Or was there something else? Finally, she swallowed and cleared her throat, daring to finally take the step.

"Dorran, I want to ask you something," she said with a straight face, as her eyes met his. Inside her heart fluttered, wavered. Skye wrestled with the words she wanted to say. "Do you think that you and I..."

Dorran's eyes shifted sideways before returning back to hers.

"Sure," he said, almost too quickly. "I'll go with you to the funeral."

The funeral? That was a million miles from what she was thinking. But strangely, a huge internal weight lifted. Without thinking she reached over and kissed him—not on the lips, but close.

"Thank you!" she said, before thinking things through. "I really appreciate it!"

"No problem."

"But you might end up regretting it."

"Really? How so?"

"Well first off, you look like Darrell. When I first saw you, I thought you were his twin. You will turn a few heads from that alone."

Dorran laughed. "Does he have this?" He lifted his right arm, showing the long snake tattoo, obvious to even the most obtuse viewer.

"No," she admitted. "But these aren't *your people*, as you've said. They'll wonder why you are with me, why they haven't met you before and why my dad never told any of them about you. And you're certain to get the fifth degree from Father."

Dorran leaned forward. "I'm not doing this for *them*. And I could care less what they think, because of my social class standing. And I'm good with that." He paused, looking almost proud. "I'm doing this for you, to support you as a friend." He reached across the table and covered her hands with his. "Okay?"

At least that was something, Skye thought. She considered how he changed the subject abruptly when she was ready to commit. Did he misunderstand her intent, or was he trying to avoid the question? Were her fears realistic, or was something else going on?

"Thank you," she replied, offering up her best smile.

Chapter 12
Ice

Dorran slid into Skye's car and snapped the seatbelt buckle in place. He gave his best reassuring smile, but he could tell it would take a lot more than that to calm her nerves.

"Good morning."

"You look nice," she said, eying him up and down. But her voice sounded far from relaxed.

He looked over his navy-blue suit and tie before glancing at her dark skirt and blouse.

"As do you," he replied. "Ready for your speech?"

"It's gonna be a short one and I can't wait until it's over."

As Skye drove along the quiet morning streets, Dorran recalled their conversation at the café the Wednesday before. He now regretted his decision to override her by changing the subject. With firm resolve he set his jaw.

"I wanted to talk about last week," he began. "From our conversation. There is something I need to tell you. Things for me recently have become... complicated."

He watched her eyes narrow and her head shake.

"Conversation?" she asked.

"You used the words, *Do you think that you and I.* I think you were going to suggest we start dating," Dorran said hesitantly. "Which I would love, believe me." He gave a nervous laugh. "But I have to go... away." It felt like all the breath left him as he spoke.

Skye pulled over at a nearby minimart and parked.

"You're going *away?*" she said, her eyes flashing. "Where? Why?"

He paused, considering how much he should tell her. Feelings of abandonment swept over him as in the past, but this time he was the one doing the leaving. Not her.

"Because of me, right?"

"No, not because of you," he said. "I wish things were different."

"I don't understand what the deal is, then," she said. "I was under the impression you weren't interested in a relationship."

"You changed my mind," Dorran said simply and honestly. "Not an easy thing to do." He hesitated, hating his welling feelings of vulnerability. But he had to know her reaction. "I've thought about you every day," he admitted. There, he said it, and relaxed as the inner pressure died down like a valve being released.

Skye turned back on the road and continued.

"And what have you been thinking about me?" she asked in a soft tone.

"How I can hardly wait to see you again," he said, looking away. "How I wish we were together."

Dorran's heart thumped through his chest as he glanced over to see Skye's mind at work, and wondering what she was thinking. Her answer would tell him what his next step would be.

"I wish we were too," she said quietly. "So, where are you going, Dorran Black?" she asked. "And for how long?"

He hated the next part, but it had to come out. He wished his circumstances were nothing more than a bad dream. "I gave the army a two-year commitment. I leave August first."

Skye nodded slightly, but her face was unreadable. "Two years," she said. "It would probably take my dad that long to get used to the idea of us dating anyway."

Dorran laughed. "So you should get to work."

"Yes, I should." She gave a sideways glance. "When did you make this decision?"

Dorran sighed. "A while back," he replied. "Before we were…friends."

She gave a slight smile. "But after I set off the fire alarm?"

Dorran was about to say no and make some excuse for her, but he wanted this relationship—whatever it turned out to be—something built on honesty.

"Yes," he said. "But I'd been considering it for almost a year before that."

"So it was my fault."

Dorran shook his head. "I came to that decision on my own, though you might have given me a slight push."

Skye nodded and wiped her eyes.

"Great."

"Skye, I have to be realistic. There is no future for me in this town. I don't have a college degree and I can't pay for a four-year university. But without that, I can't raise a family here. Max has been great, but there's only so much he can do for me. The army will give me training and help pay for school."

"What do you want to do with your training?" Her voice was a soft whisper.

"Run my own auto shop," he said. "A dream I've had for a long time."

Skye pulled her BMW over once again, but this time on a wide shoulder.

"I need you to drive," she said. "Got some more prep work for my speech."

*

The Coeur d'Alene Community Church stood tall, expansive and white, with a red cross stretched along one side and a steeple reaching skyward. The parking lot, which was mostly full, boasted a couple acres of space.

Dorran followed the directions of the parking attendants until he found a spot beneath a tall maple tree. He looked over at Skye, who wrote furiously on a small piece of paper, folded it up and stuffed it inside her purse.

She nodded and together they walked inside the building.

Organ music played Pachelbel's Canon in D Major as Dorran and Skye entered the foyer behind dozens of other people, dressed in black or navy blue. An elderly bald man handed each of them a funeral program.

Dorran's face slackened as he scanned the cover: a picture of Darrell with his name beneath, along with the words *In Loving Memory* at the top. It was like looking into a mirror. Only his hair was slightly longer.

"Told you," Skye said quietly as their eyes met.

"Yep," he replied, grinding his teeth. "You did."

Hundreds of people sat in the main sanctuary of the church, waiting for the service to begin. Dorran paused as his eyes quickly searched for room near the back.

Skye took his right arm. "Not so lucky," she whispered. "We have reserved seating. Second row."

Dorran choked. "That close?" he blurted a little too loud, and heads turned his way.

"Oh, my god!" cried a woman on his left. She looked directly at him, eyes wide.

This, of course set those around her to also stare in Dorran's direction, and in seconds a bunch of murmurs and whispers filled the air. Some shook their heads. Others covered their faces.

"That can't be him."

"They look so alike!"

"Is this a joke?"

"Did he have a twin?"

"Maybe it's his ghost."

As Dorran felt his face burn, he did his best to look straight ahead as Skye gripped his arm tighter than ever, helping him move forward, against his very strong inner urging to exit the premises right then and there.

Unfortunately, the clamor did not subside. In fact, the talk swelled with each row they passed. Several young voices exclaimed, "That's Darrell!" before being hushed by their parents or grandparents, or some other adult. But they all stared.

One little girl could not be so easily silenced. "Well, he sure looks like him!" she shouted to her mother.

By the time Dorran and Skye reached the second row, hundreds of eyes were on them. The buzzing of the crowd drowned out the organ.

Skye's anxious-looking father and mother turned their heads with the rest of the crowd, and when Charles Larson leaned forward, Skye whispered loudly as she sat next to him.

"This is Dorran, the mechanic." Charles stared at her for a moment before he nodded and looked behind him. At once, some of the voices died away.

Those in the first row, however, stared intently at Dorran, including a couple who sat immediately ahead, and whose faces were filled with tears and confusion. Dorran guessed they were Darrell's parents.

Skye leaned forward.

"I am so sorry, Mr. and Mrs. Cargill. This is my friend, Dorran."

The couple nodded in unison and turned back around. Two other men, some years older than Darrell, looked at them a while longer before sitting forward again.

"Darrell's cousins," Skye whispered.

As the organ faded, Dorran noted the closed casket directly in front. It was large, fancy and served as a strong reminder that Darrell Cargill was indeed, dead.

The music stopped, and an elderly clergyman in a dark suit took his place behind the pulpit and spoke into the mic. He led the crowd to stand and pray over Darrell and his family. From there he spoke of Darrell's life and accomplishments.

Dorran watched Skye tense as she read through her notes. Dorran looked over the flyer and realized she was next to speak.

Finally, the clergyman finished and introduced Skye, who held a folded paper in her shaking hand. As she stepped in front of Dorran, she pressed a much smaller piece of paper into his left hand before walking onto the stage. Dorran, conscious of Charles Larson's stare, kept his hand closed and turned his focus on the beautiful and brave girl he so wanted to be with at that moment. He didn't care if everyone watched him, if he could just be there right now, holding her hand through what must be one of the most difficult moments of her life. It sure beat sitting on a pew by himself with a crowd of strangers wondering if he was Darrell back from the dead.

"Thank you for coming," Skye spoke into the microphone. "To celebrate Darrell's life." Her eyes began to shine and her hands shook as she opened her paper. "There are many things I could say, but I chose to write a poem instead."

Skye glanced quickly at Dorran as she began reading. She spoke slowly, deliberately, emphasizing every word as if the meaning of each was priceless. As she read, sniffles spread throughout the sanctuary, with many women holding handkerchiefs to their eyes.

It seems like just yesterday
Our paths crossed,
Iron striking iron.
You the Immovable Object,
Me the Irresistible Force.
Until I saw that Something in you that
caught
more than my Eye.
It snared my Heart.

The words perplexed Dorran. Was this what she really thought of Darrell? Whenever she spoke of him before, it was as if he was the scum of the earth, instead of a god who died too early. Was she required to write something like this in order to appease Darrell's family, or Skye's dad? Or did she really mean those words?

But Time was against us
And all at once our Chance at Life
together Vanished
Like sand Flowing through my fingers.

As sobs rose from the crowd, Dorran slowly and unobtrusively unfolded the small piece of paper in his hand. Maybe her note would hold some clue to the meaning of her words.

The first poem I wrote for you. The second was written for us.

Dorran choked but covered it up with a faint cough as he quickly refolded the paper and stuffed it inside his jacket pocket. He cursed himself for signing up with the army as his previous plans now no longer held any attraction. He wanted to be with Skye, to share his future with her.

It seemed like half the crowd was crying by now, and Skye wiped her eyes as she continued.

"I would like to share one more poem. This one written by Henry Van Dyke."

Time is...
Too slow for those who wait,
Too swift for those who fear,
Too long for those who grieve,
Too short for those who rejoice;
But for those who love,
Time is not.

Tears flowed in the church. Even Skye's father seemed to have something in his eye, though he made no noise, unlike Adelaide, who sobbed almost constantly.

After Skye returned to her place in the pew, Dorran squeezed her hand and gave her an appreciative nod. He remembered little of the remaining service. His thoughts focused on the poems she read aloud. They might have appeared to be for Darrell, but Dorran was over the moon inside.

Because those words were for him.

Chapter 13
Fire

Adelaide smiled across the dining room table.

"Skye, your father and I thought you did a wonderful job at the funeral today, didn't we dear?"

Charles looked up from his small bowl of chocolate pudding and nodded. "I wasn't aware that you and Darrell were that close," he said. "But yes, you represented the family very well. We are proud of you, as always."

Skye simply stared at her dessert, not feeling any urge to eat. The country club meal following the funeral filled her for the rest of the day.

"My, but your friend Dorran certainly caused a stir, didn't he?" her mother added, snapping Skye to attention.

Skye looked at Adelaide without expression.

"What do you mean?" she asked in her most innocent fashion. "I thought he behaved himself very well."

Her mother laughed. "I mean he looked so much like Darrell, it had people wondering. Did he do it on purpose?"

Skye shrugged. "He never met Darrell, so I doubt it."

"Why was Dorran with you today?" Charles asked in a casual sounding voice.

But Skye knew it was anything but a casual question. "He could tell I was upset after I heard about Darrell's death," she explained. "After I told him what happened, he offered to go with me."

"But why?" Charles pressed, his face turning a darker shade. "You say he never met the boy, yet he was willing to go with you to his funeral?"

Skye looked at her father, her face hardening slightly. "He wanted to support me on a very difficult day."

The man nodded as he sighed and leaned back. "That is all well and good, I suppose. Nothing wrong with it, of course. But I don't want him thinking that he is going to be able to take advantage of this situation."

"What do you mean?" Skye asked, again using her innocent voice. Inside, she simmered.

"He fixed your car, which means a great deal to you. And yes, I admit he did a very fine job with it. But if he changed his appearance to look like Darrell, he might use that to initiate some sort of romance."

"Oh dear," Adelaide said with a laugh. "I think it's all quite innocent. The boy is simply being kind to her, that is all. Right, Skye?"

Skye's mind shifted to Dorran, remembering the look of longing in his eyes—for her alone. He seemed overprotective as they left the church, always keeping his arm around her, not allowing anyone else to come too close. It was a good thing her parents did not see that. But who else had?

"Skye? Are you all right?" her mother asked.

"What?" she asked, realizing she was smiling.

"I was just saying that Dorran was being kind to you, like a friend would."

"I suppose," she said reluctantly. "Like a good friend."

"He didn't join us for lunch afterward," her mom said. "I would have liked to speak with him."

"As I think a lot of people would," Skye replied. "But as I said before, he was there to support me during the funeral, not answer a lot of personal questions about his appearance."

Charles cleared his throat.

"As long as it doesn't become something else, I see no problem," Charles said.

"Become something else?" Skye asked, using all the energy inside her to mask her real feelings.

The man laughed and shook his head. "Sometimes I think you can be a little on the naïve side, Skye," he said with an added chuckle. "Someone like Dorran would never fit properly in our family—you know that. It's simply a matter of upbringing, training, and a host of other things that is required in our family businesses."

"Though I do sometimes wonder if my future husband might not be interested in our family businesses. What if he wanted a business of his own?" In her mind Skye envisioned Dorran owning and working in his own auto repair shop.

"That's why we screen all the potentials out there," Charles said. "To make the very best fit. There are hundreds, perhaps thousands of possibilities, but we only want the right one for you."

"So, I don't get to choose?" Skye asked with a slight smile. She glanced over at her mother, who stared down at her plate.

"Of course you get to choose," Charles said jovially, with a sideways glance at his wife. "We've brought you up so you will be able, in time, to pick the right man." He chuckled again and shook his head. "Though I don't know how this subject came up all of a sudden," he said. "There's lots of time before you ever need to worry about that."

Skye simply nodded.

"However, I think it proper for you to limit your interactions with this, uh, *mechanic,* so he doesn't start getting the wrong idea about you. His job is done with the car, so there really is no reason for you to see him again, is there?"

"Not really," she answered with a shrug, keeping her face relaxed as if she didn't care one bit.

"Now dear, I don't see how it could hurt," Adelaide interjected with a worried smile. "Skye's working so hard she hardly has any social time this summer. It will take time to get over Darrell's death, so now may not be the right time for her to be looking for anyone else. I think it is all quite innocent to have a friend like Dorran."

Skye glanced at her mom and shook her head.

"No, he's right. I don't want to give Dorran any false impressions. It wouldn't be fair to him."

She looked back at her father, who beamed at her with pride. But her mother looked stricken.

*

Skye lay back in her king-size bed, phone in her ear, staring at the expansive decorated ceiling.

"*I miss you,*" came Dorran's husky, sexy voice.

"I miss you too," she said softly. "What's on your agenda for this week?"

"*Lots of car parts coming in at work,*" he said. "*For the F-150 and the Jeep. That should keep me busy right up until the end. But I wanted to invite you to an early dinner.*"

Skye sat straight up, her heart suddenly kicking in high gear. "Yes?" she asked.

"*Finn and his parents are getting together at Angelo's, Saturday at four. Want to come?*"

"Of course," Skye replied. "I'd love to meet them. Didn't you say you knew the Parkers in Denver?"

"Yeah, they're like the family I never had. I can't wait to introduce you."

"Probably like the family I never had either," Skye mused.

Dorran's laugh came through the phone. "*You're gonna love 'em, I promise!*"

*

"Skye! So nice to meet you!"

Skye was enveloped in a bear hug by Lisa Parker, a tall and energetic 44-year-old woman, with sandy blond hair and glasses.

"Thank you!" Skye managed to say, taken aback by this show of affection from someone she didn't know.

Brian Parker, a 46-year-old balding man with short, black hair and round glasses, acted more reserved. He simply took her hand in his.

"How are you, Skye?" Brian said with a smile.

The Angelo's Ristorante host led the group to a large round table where Finn and his parents sat first. After Skye took a seat, Dorran slid in next to her.

The spacious room boasted a quiet atmosphere, with soft orange hanging lamps, white tablecloths and dark carpets. Even at this hour between lunch and dinner, the place was mostly full.

Lisa Parker simply beamed. "We don't see Dorran as often anymore, so this is truly a special occasion."

"Still at least once a month, Mom," Finn countered, while glancing at his menu. For the first time, Skye took full notice of him, realizing there were now two gorgeous hunks at the table instead of just one. Finn had more of a styled, relaxed look like James Dean, but with longer, parted hair. He was every bit as muscular as Dorran, if not more. Skye wondered if he was single and thought of Sage.

Lisa smiled at Finn. "Oh, I know. It just seems longer than that." She turned to Skye. "Dorran tells me you go to Stanford. What's your major?"

"Economics," she replied. "But I'm thinking of changing it to advertising."

"Sounds interesting," Brian said. "What do you want to do with it?"

"You've heard of Arrowroot Bakery?" Dorran asked.

"Of course," Lisa said with a nod. "Radio, TV, it's everywhere. I've been meaning to get over there. I heard they have gluten free cupcakes!"

"Meet the brains behind all of that," Dorran said, pointing in Skye's direction. Then he gently took her hand and squeezed.

Lisa's face turned in surprise. "Skye, that is wonderful!" she exclaimed. "You are definitely in your element. Those commercials are genius!"

Skye found herself genuinely embarrassed with all the compliments and her face heated up. Fortunately, she didn't have to respond because the waiter showed up, ready to take their order.

After the Parkers ordered, the waiter turned to Skye.

"I'll have whatever Dorran picks," she said, not having a chance to read the menu.

Dorran ordered a dish of chicken, noodles and cream sauce, with milk to drink. Skye changed her drink to a coke.

Lisa looked Dorran.

"Still having ulcers?"

Dorran's face colored but he shrugged easily. Skye knew this was his knee jerk reaction to an unexpected question. But he always managed to cover it up.

"Sometimes," he said. "But it's under control."

After some chat about the weather and how this July seemed hotter than last year, Lisa abruptly changed the topic of conversation and looked at Dorran.

"When do you ship out?"

"August first."

Finn's mom sucked in her breath. "Two weeks? That soon? We're gonna miss you, Dorran!" She started to tear up. "You know you're like a son to us."

Finn gave his James Dean deadpan look. "Mom, I think he knows he's part of our family."

But Brian reached over and squeezed Lisa's hand.

"So how did you meet Dorran?" Skye asked, hoping to break up the uncomfortable emotion of the moment.

Lisa brightened. "Finn and Dorran were friends in school back in Denver. Sometimes we'd catch up with his parents." Then her smile faded. "So, when things got tough for his family, we sort of took him in and he's been ours ever since!"

Skye glanced over at Dorran to see his eyes shining. This surprised her, as she'd never seen that before. Typically he kept everything so tight inside it was hard to figure out what he was thinking. But not now. It was as if a chink just appeared in his impenetrable armor.

"I think that's awesome!" Skye complimented Lisa. "So, you moved here together?"

Lisa nodded. "After they finished high school Brian and I applied for the open x-ray tech and nurse positions at Kootenai Medical. Finn and Dorran have been working at Max's ever since. What is it, going on three years now?"

Finn nodded and smiled at Skye with folded arms. "And I taught him everything he knows."

Everyone laughed at that, especially Dorran.

Brian cleared his throat. "We are proud of you, Dorran, and know you will do well wherever you go. The army is lucky to have you."

"Hear! Hear!" Finn said, raising his glass of light beer. Everyone else raised their glasses and toasted to Dorran.

"Thank you," he replied quietly. His face turned serious like he was intensely uncomfortable.

"Where are you reporting?" Brian asked.

"Fort Jackson, South Carolina," he said in a voice that lacked excitement. He glanced at Skye. "For ten weeks."

Chapter 14
Ice

Dorran sped along Ramsey Park Trail, a popular six-mile, scenic running loop near town. It was early morning, the sunlight just starting to steam along the heavily dewed ground. He completed over half the route when his cell phone vibrated: a text from someone he knew. Like Skye. But it was Sunday morning. The Arrowroot Bakery would be closed. Why would she call this early?

His mood rose as he slowed and sat on a nearby bench. He pulled out his phone, but the message wasn't from Skye. It was from someone in his past who rarely sent good news.

He read a text several times, not wanting to believe.

Renée is in ICU. OD'd last night on opioids.

Hot tears threatened as he gasped for air and his emotions turned dark. He looked again at the messenger's ID. He didn't want the conversation but there was no avoiding.

He dialed the source number.

"What's up?" came the rough voice on the other end.

"Hey Dick," Dorran said quietly.

"That's Uncle Richard to you."

"Oh, yeah," Dorran replied. He paused. "So, what happened with Renée?"

"Not a hundred percent sure. Last night she acted upset about something, which is normal. But she wouldn't talk. Also normal. This morning we found her. To be honest I thought you'd be the first to go."

"What do you mean? Is she dead?" His heart sped up.

"No. I didn't mean it that way. I just mean I thought you'd do something this stupid before she did."

Dorran ignored the insult. "Where is she?" he pressed, his stress mounting.

"Saint Joseph. Where else?"

"Okay, I'm on my way."

"Hold on, Mr. Knight-In-Shining-Armor." The man let off a few chuckles. *"No one is allowed to see her for a few days, so just cool your dets."*

"My dets?" Dorran asked, scowling. "You been drinking again?"

"So what if I have?" It sounded like he gave out a snort. "*You are in no position to judge me! Not after what you did. So just watch your mouth.*"

"Okay, fine. I'm just upset, that's all."

"As are we all, Dorran."

"So why can't anyone see her?"

"This is how it works. They don't know what happened and them allowing folks in just might make it worse, see? They say she should be fine, so don't get your tighty whitey's in a twist. That's all I know. After three days they'll move her to detox."

"Where?"

"Tri Star."

Gloom and darkness descended. Dorran's only sister was stuck in a hospital room two states away and he wasn't there to help. He closed his eyes, trying to push away the depression. But guilt mixed in as he knew he made the choice to live this far away.

A minute passed.

"You still there? Look, I gotta get to work so—"

Dorran hit the red phone icon. Dick hadn't held a job since he was laid off years ago, so he wasn't going to accept that as an excuse to part conversation.

He stared at the still-moist ground. The small pebbles in the dark soil. Loneliness took him for a few seconds before he thought of Skye and dialed.

She picked up on the second ring. Her sleepy voice sounded.

"What's up?"

Dorran's mind went blank. How could he start this conversation? What should he tell her? Things were bad enough since he was leaving in 11 days. Why amp up the pressure?

"Dorran?" Her voice sounded worried. *"I can hear you breathing. Are you hurt? What happened? Where are you?"*

"I'm...I'm fine," he said finally, trying to reassure. "I just got some bad news."

"Where are you?"

"Ramsey Park Trail. Fifth bench."

"I know it. Be there in a few."

*

"Dorran."

Skye sat beside him, arm around his shoulder. He stared blankly at the ground, his body weighed down by grief and guilt. All he could do was show her the text message.

But she took it well. After working over her own phone, she turned to him.

"Okay, I've cleared my schedule. I'll check the next flight to Denver."

He looked into her beautiful, partially-wet eyes and smiled.

"Seriously?"

"Of course. I know how important sisters are."

Dorran sat back and shrugged.

"My uncle said no one can see her for a few days, so I'll probably just take my bike."

"I can go with you."

"Probably not the best idea."

Skye pulled back, frowning.

"And why is that?"

Dorran rubbed his hands together but wouldn't look at her.

"I don't want to cause waves with your family."

Skye was quiet until he looked into her mesmerizing eyes.

"What did my dad say to you?"

Dorran shook his head slightly. "It wasn't him. Someone who works for him, though. Wally...Walter...someone."

Skye sighed quickly. "Wallace. My *butt*-ler."

Dorran snapped his fingers and gave a bitter smile. "Yep, Wallace. Said I shouldn't be calling you up or bothering you anymore." Dorran grinned. "He wasn't rude."

"Why didn't you tell me?"

Dorran took her hand, admiringly.

"He doesn't scare me. I can handle myself. But if you go with me...you'll be miserable much longer than the eleven days we have left."

"I don't care about that," she said quietly. Her expression was pained, as if he hurt her intentionally. Immediately he regretted even calling her.

"I'm sorry, Skye. I shouldn't have bothered you with this."

Her expression changed to something more resolute.

"You are important to me, so your family is important to me," she said, her voice tinged with anger. "Wallace just needs to pull his fat nose out of my business."

Dorran laughed. "Speaking of sisters, how is Liliane?"

"Wondering when the other shoe will drop with you," Skye replied with a mischievous look. "She says you must have a dark past you are hiding, no one can be that perfect, etcetera. Otherwise you'd have been married off by now."

Dorran laughed again. "Perfect? Is that how you described me?"

"No, not in those exact words," she replied, stealing a kiss. "Just the perfect one for me."

Dorran kissed her fully back and she responded in kind. His senses went into high gear until he brought them back under control and pulled away gently.

"So, she hates me?" he asked with a gasp. But it was a happy gasp.

Skye laughed. "Why don't you ask her yourself?"

Dorran pretended to shrink back. "Oh no. Meet the sister? Way too much stress there. She's like, what, thirty?"

"Yeah, so?"

"Too much adult in her. I don't stand a chance."

Skye met his glance with a mischievous smile. "So tell me more about your sister."

"Renée? She turns 17 on Thursday, and I was planning on seeing her next weekend. She'll graduate high school next year. Said she wanted to start her own *Jackass* movie."

"Jackass? The one where the idiots get bashed up and almost killed?"

"That's the one." Dorran laughed. "She's always been the trickster type. She can think up some real funny stunts too. But she says Jackass was too tame and she wanted to *improve* on it."

Skye smiled and nodded politely. "So...what happened to her?"

"No one seems to know. Something upset her last night but she wouldn't talk."

"She lives with your uncle?"

Dorran nodded. "And my aunt. She's been with them since she was ten."

"But they never took you in?"

Dorran's face heated, realizing how little she knew about his past.

"I...ahh...had other arrangements," he said. "It wasn't a good time for anyone."

"Want to talk about it?" she asked. "We have a family therapist."

Dorran stared. "You have a family therapist?"

She deadpanned. "Obviously you don't know my family well enough. If you did, you wouldn't be surprised. But anytime you want to talk, I could set up an appointment."

"Thanks." Dorran shook his head. "But I don't have that kind of money."

Skye laughed. "It won't cost you a dime. We have so much credit built up with so many missed visits that she owes us for

163

years. But my mom keeps sending the monthly check."

Dorran imagined himself laying on a couch, telling a perfect stranger his whole life story. He shuddered involuntarily.

Not gonna happen.

"I'll think about it," he lied.

Skye reflected a look of strong disbelief. "Okay, well. Are we going to finish your run before your legs cramp up? I brought a change of clothes."

Dorran's spirits lifted. "Sure. Race you there?"

*

Dorran didn't want the run to stop. Skye kept up with him easily to the end of the trail, and when they backtracked to the bench.

Both sat, Dorran breathing heavier.

"What are your plans today?" he asked, holding his side. Either a stitch or stomach upset, he couldn't tell.

Skye pulled out her phone and stood.

"Breakfast with Sage and Olivia. Then my mom wanted help with some landscaping. After that, check over some new ads for the store."

"Busy day." His mood darkened, wishing she could be with him for the entire day instead of leaving himself to his dark thoughts.

"Walk me to the car?" she asked.

Chapter 15
Fire

Skye reclined on the light brown Burrow Nomad Sofa, looking up at the vaulted ceiling with its huge dark brown beams. Her face relaxed.

Marjorie gave a twisted smile. "So how is your Monday morning?"

"A lot better than the last time I was here."

The woman gave Skye a look. "You mean now that Darrell is gone?"

Skye sat up. "What? No, I wasn't even thinking about him. Whatever possesses you to think that way?"

The woman shrugged, her face sagging. "So sorry. Habit I suppose." She cleared her throat. "So, what's the topic of the day?"

Skye held up two fingers.

"Oh my, a breakthrough," the woman said with a laugh. "For that many, I think I'll need another cup of tea."

"So funny. But this is serious. Are you up for it?"

"As always, my dear. Fire away."

"And confidential."

Marjorie sighed. "Really Skye, your mistrust does start to wear at times."

"I'm here, aren't I?"

Another sigh. "Of course. Yes, as per usual all of our conversations are held in the strictest confidence."

"All right then," she said. "My dad and Dorran."

"Are these issues interrelated or isolated?"

"Intertwined, unfortunately. The spies have been working overtime again."

"I take it you mean Wallace?"

Now it was Skye's turn to sigh. "Wallace, the cook, the maids, you name it. I swear they are worse than the paparazzi."

"How so?"

"I want to be with Dorran, but Father doesn't approve. Says he'll never fit in, doesn't have the right upbringing, character, morals, and so forth. So of course that puts everyone on alert to my aberrant behavior. I have to be careful where I go or any phone call I make in case someone listens in on my conversation."

A moment of silence ensued.

"What happened, Skye?" Marjorie asked in a professional, soft tone.

"Wallace happened. Probably saw us together, or overheard a conversation. It doesn't matter who, but I can't trust anyone at home anymore. Except Marcus. Actually, it doesn't even feel like home."

"Marcus, your driver?"

"Yes, Marcus who used to be the butler until Wallace essentially uprooted him and took his place. I'm surprised Marcus stayed around after that, but I remember Liliane begging him not to leave."

"So what did your father say to you this time?"

"Oh, the standard." She lowered her voice. "As long as you are in my house, eating my food, taking my money for your school, you will obey the house rules." She paused. "Same thing he said to Liliane years ago, not long before she left."

"And so you think the cycle is repeating itself."

Skye nodded. "I know it is. But I don't want to be my sister. It would kill Mother, and my world as I know it would explode in flames."

"So has your mother said anything about your relationship with Dorran?"

"No, but she always agrees with Father. I think sometimes she wants to say something but she never does."

"Let's go to the other topic of conversation," Marjorie said. "Dorran. Tell me about him."

Skye felt her heart speed up as she lay back down on the very comfortable couch. He made her feel important. He was strong and steady, not juvenile and scattered. He acted like she was the most important thing in the world when she was with him. But not one of these words would she share with her counselor.

"It's my fault he is leaving for the military."

"What?" Marjorie cried as if caught off guard. "What on earth would give him sane reason to do that? And why is this all your fault?"

"He has good reasons," Skye replied quietly. "He needs training so he can run his own business one day. He's very good at fixing cars—you should see mine now. Better than new."

"Better than new?" Marjorie's words dripped with disbelief.

"After our session I'll show you."

"All right, I would like that," she replied. "But blaming yourself for his decision is simply illogical, my dear. If he does it to improve his life, I would think you should be happy for him."

"He'll be gone for two years," Skye said so quietly amidst her eyes watering. "I don't know what I will do without him."

Marjorie put her pen down. Skye saw her bring a handkerchief to one eye and dab. "So what are you planning to do?" she finally asked.

Skye sat up on her arms and sniffed. "That's your purpose—to help guide me to a logical and mature decision."

Marjorie sat ramrod straight. "I will do my best, though you're probably not going to like what I have to say."

"Wouldn't be the first time."

Marjorie snorted. "Listen, Skye, I know you've been playing the game with your parents. You don't want a repeat of the Great Meltdown that happened with Liliane. Lord knows nobody wants that. However, hiding behind the good girl act isn't any better, and it will implode one day."

Skye stared at her. "Then what do you think I should do?"

Marjorie folded her arms. "Be honest with them. Tell them what you want. What you really want. That will let your father and mother know where you stand and they will respect you for it."

"Father will likely restrict any freedom I still have. That's what he did with Liliane."

"Try to help them understand from your point of view. What does Dorran mean to you? How you see your life with him in the future?"

Skye sat up, open-mouthed. "They would kill me!"

Marjorie laughed. "I doubt that, being as you are the sole heir of the estate. But this will take time—years most likely, until they understand you have a will of your own and compromise is required to make this all work."

Skye lay back down, shaking her head. Marjorie's advice sounded like the very opposite of what she should do. Every fiber of her being screamed against it.

*

Skye sat back on one of the old and comfy couches at Calypsos Coffee. After setting down her mug of *Americano*, she dialed her sister.

"This is Liliane," came the voice through the phone.

"What's up, Sis?" Skye said. "Long time no talk."

There was a snort. *"Yeah, like two days ago. How's Marjorie?"*

"She always gets this faraway look in her eyes whenever we talk about you."

"I'll bet. She's probably never gotten over losing me as a client. I think I made her a million dollars during my rebellious years. A pause. *Are you at Calypsos on a week night?"*

"Yep."

"So the spies are abroad?"

"Every one of them."

"Well, watch your back. Especially around Wallace. That place was a snake pit back in my day, but you never know. It could be worse now." A pause. *"So what's up?"*

"Dorran and Dad."

There was silence on the other end for a few uncomfortable moments. Then a long sigh.

"Screw Dad. Do what you want. Don't let him rule your life."

Skye smiled to herself. That sounded like her sister.

"Besides, Dorran's only going to be here a few more days and that's it, right? If I were you I'd spend as much time with him as I could. Dad will get over it. Then when Dorran gets back, you'll be out of school and you can live your own life."

"I can't wait two years and keep pretending Dorran is out of my life. Besides, he'll probably find someone else."

"Not likely. If Dorran is the type I think he is, he'll miss you just as much and won't think of changing partners. You guys can make it work. I wish I did with James. Dad was a jerk back then and he's a jerk now. Some things—and people--never change."

"Marjorie's advice was that I get all honest and tell both Dad and Mom my feelings for Dorran."

A loud guffaw sounded on the other end. "Well now, that sounds like a repeat of what I tried, though I was a bit more dramatic than you would probably be. And I do remember throwing a few plates and chairs around."

"I remember. So how is James?"

A sob and sigh. "Married with a couple of kids. Moved to Portland and works for Boeing. Earned his way through school just like I thought he would."

Tears came to Skye's eyes. "Sorry, I didn't know. I was hoping he would wait for you."

A laugh. *"Father scared him. Bad. Or maybe it was Wallace. He would never say exactly what happened, but it was a long time before he would ever talk to me. By then he found his wife."*

"Dorran said Wallace talked to him but he didn't seem upset about it."

Several swear words later, Liliane seemed to calm down. *"Listen to me Skye, Father will not stop until Dorran is out of your life. Completely. I wish I had known that before and maybe things could have been different with me and James. But if you're not very careful the same thing is going to happen."* A sigh. *"But I have a few ideas if you want to listen."*

Skye's heart sped up.

"Absolutely!"

Chapter 16
Ice

Thursday morning Skye met Dorran as he pulled his '69 Honda CB750 from Max's garage. He wore a medium-sized backpack for the trip.

Skye's dress seemed overly casual, with faded blue jeans, pink t-shirt and Converse sneakers.

"We're almost a matched set," Dorran said with a smile. "Except for my leather jacket. And green shirt."

Skye's face showed no emotion as she handed him a large bag labeled *Arrowroot Bakery*. She leaned forward, tip-toed upward, and planted a full kiss on his lips. He responded in kind and took her fully in his arms. After embracing for what felt like almost enough time, Skye pulled back with a smile. She glanced at his bag.

"For your trip," she said.

"I sort of figured," he replied softly. "Thanks."

"What route are you taking?"

"Interstate 90 to 25," he replied, now wishing she was going with him. "I should get there by tomorrow night. I'll call you."

Skye nodded slightly. "Okay. Drive safe."

Dorran started his bike and tucked her sack into his backpack before swinging it back onto his back. After sliding on his helmet, he nodded once and waved.

His stomach hurt a little as he made his way through Sherman Avenue and out of Coeur d'Alene. Sometimes the pain came from eating the wrong thing, though he tended to be careful now that he had plenty of digestion experience gone wrong. Other times it was nerves or lack of sleep. This time he guessed it was one of the latter.

Once on Interstate 90, Dorran made good time after the morning rush hour traffic. He thought about Skye, part of him wishing she was with him right now, the other part not wanting to get her into trouble. He knew families like hers could make life miserable. The last thing he wanted was for her to end up like her sister Liliane.

With only about a week remaining before he reported to Fort Jackson, South Carolina, Dorran knew that every hour he spent with her was precious. He'd make it up to her when he got back and spend every waking minute possible with her. He just hoped she wouldn't forget about him when he was gone.

The day grew warm but the route was scenic, taking Dorran through mountains, forests and pretty valleys. He stopped at a park in Pinehurst and ate a few of the rolls from Arrowroot Bakery. He savored the flavors, appreciating what this food did for his stomach instead of to it.

As the day wore on and Dorran tired, his mind focused less on being with Skye and more on a recent conversation with Wallace, the Larson family butler. He remembered almost every word of it and it replayed in his mind.

"Is Mr. Dorran Black available?"

"Speaking."

"Hello Mr. Black. My name is Wallace Livingston, and I represent the Charles Larson estate. Do you have a few minutes to talk?"

Dorran had wished he had a good excuse not to, and he dreaded what was to come. But it wasn't unexpected.

"Yes I do, Mr. Livingston. But please call me Dorran."

"Thank you, Dorran. And first of all, Mr. Larson wanted to congratulate you on the stellar work you performed on Skye's car. He said it did not seem possible that this was the very same vehicle that was involved in the car crash just over a month ago."

A pause ensued.

"Thank you," Dorran said politely.

"Mr. Larson also wanted to know if you received your bonus for the work."

Another pause.

"Yes, I did."

"Very good and glad to hear it. You certainly earned it. Mr. Larson also wanted to convey his appreciation for your support during Darrell Cargill's funeral. There was certainly no obligation on your part to be there and he hopes it did not cause you any undue stress."

"I thought that Skye could use the support, given everything she has been through."

"Of course, and again Mr. Larson wanted to convey his sincere appreciation."

This time Dorran let the pause linger.

"And so this brings me to the point of our conversation, Dorran. We've noticed *that you are spending a lot of time with Skye, both in person and on the phone."*

Dorran chose his words carefully.

"She is a good friend."

"It seems as if the relationship is going beyond friendship. And that is what I need to speak with you about."

"Oh?" Dorran said, trying to keep his voice calm.

"We realize that Skye cares about you, but you must understand our position in this relationship."

Dorran knew fully what their position was, but he wanted to let Wallace tell him fully.

"Oh?" he asked, again keeping his voice monotone.

"Yes, you see, Mr. Larson owns several businesses and Skye is his sole heir. In order to ensure that these businesses succeed in the future, we feel it is in Skye's best interest to choose someone who will align himself with the goals of the Larson Estate."

Dorran could not think of anything decent to say.

"But as compensation for your investment in her life, Mr. Larson is willing to grant you, shall we say, a severance fee."

"A severance fee?"

179

"Yes. If you are willing to end your relationship with Miss Larson, the estate will pay you $100,000. Under the table, of course."

Dorran's eyes widened at the amount. He imagined a good down payment on a house, traveling the globe, buying a lot of different and wonderful things. But his mind quickly came back to earth when Wallace spoke again.

"Mr. Black, are you still there?"

"Yes, Mr. Livingston. I am."

"I wanted to impress upon you the importance of this matter. If you choose not to end your relationship with Miss Larson, then I am afraid things could go, shall I say, 'south'?"

"Oh?" Dorran said, his tone turning sharp.

"Dorran, I hate to bring up your past, but I wanted to let you know that I recently learned about your father's imprisonment, your mother's disappearance, and your own criminal record. You can see how this could adversely affect Skye if this news broke out around Coeur d'Alene."

Dorran's anger almost got the best of him, but he knew better. Experience taught him to be cold, unfeeling in situations like this. That was the only real weapon he had.

"I see your point, Mr. Livingston," he said. "I will have to think about this. But—and please don't take this wrong, but I could never accept what I consider in this case to be a bribe. This would be of my own free will, with no strings attached."

This time there was a long pause.

"Of course, and thank you for being forthright. And we ask that you do not mention the contents of this conversation with Miss Larson or else it could make things... complicated."

"I understand," Dorran said.

"Mr. Larson also wanted to congratulate you on your up and coming entry into the United States Army. He wishes you the best of success there. He also has strong ties with the military in case you ever need a recommendation."

"I will keep that in mind, Mr. Livingston." Another veiled threat that almost pushed Dorran to the edge, but he'd been expecting it. Mr. Larson could make things go well or very badly for him, depending on his decision about Skye.

"Thank you for your understanding, Mr. Black. Please call back within a few days to the number on your phone. Good bye."

Around three that afternoon, the sun was hidden by some large, dark clouds. It was still a few hours to his hotel in Billings, Montana and his stomach growled in hunger. But his mind stayed absorbed with that fateful phone call. Although glad he kept his cool with Wallace, he knew any future with her would be difficult. In order to protect Skye, they would have to be very careful every time they were together or had even a simple phone conversation. Or would it be better if he walked away? But his heart rebelled at that thought.

Dorran turned off at Bozeman for his mid-afternoon meal. He found *Red Tractor Pizza*, where he enjoyed a delicious gluten free pepperoni pizza. He waited inside the restaurant for almost an hour, until a thunderstorm passed by, before he was back on the road.

But his mind couldn't drop the conversation with Wallace, and his thoughts soon put him into a near depression. He used all his remaining energy to focus on the wet and misty road, but it wasn't enough. While making his way out of Bozeman he missed seeing the four deer jump in front of him until it was too late.

Chapter 17
Fire

The manor's grand entry doors opened before Skye, where Wallace, the short black man with a head of silvering hair waited for her. But this time he wore no dazzling smile.

"Good evening, Miss Larson," he said evenly.

She looked at him, immediately suspicious. Something happened and she wondered if it had something to do with her and Dorran.

"Good evening," she replied wistfully.

Wallace opened the tall, chestnut dining hall doors, where Skye could see her parents at the end of the immaculate table, waiting. Her father, dressed in his typical dark business suit, sat in his usual place at the head, while Adelaide sat on his left.

"Skye," Charles Larson said as he stood tall on his feet. "Glad you could make it." Adelaide stood as well, revealing a black dinner dress. But she did not smile.

"Hello Father... Mother," she replied. "Sorry I'm late. Got caught up at work." They greeted each other with a kiss on the cheek. "Have a good day?"

Charles peered at her. "I've had better. What about you?"

"Like any other day I suppose," she returned with a slight smile as they sat. "The Arrowroot Bakery's success continues."

Skye thought her mother would respond to that but she looked straight ahead as if she heard nothing.

Wallace, standing a few feet behind them, cleared his throat. "Tonight's main selection is Mongolian beef over steamed rice," he announced. "Potato skins or wedge salad-on-a-stick as your appetizers and chocolate cheesecake for dessert."

"Very good Wallace," Charles replied. "I will have the potato skins."

"Potato skins for me as well," Adelaide said. She smiled at her husband, still not looking at Skye.

"Wedge salad," Skye replied deliberately.

Her mother finally turned to her and laughed. "I thought you hated that appetizer."

Skye shrugged. "People change," she said politely.

Wallace nodded slightly. "Very good," he said as he turned and left for the kitchen.

Adelaide looked to Charles, her habit of total attention focused once again on him. But her expression was sad, depressed.

"How was your day, dear?" she asked quietly.

"Mixed," came his reply, his large hands twitching. "The DOW was up over 300 points and the S&P up 70. The NASDAQ climbed 55 at the bell."

"How did our stocks do, Father?" Skye asked in her gentle, practiced voice.

Charles peered at her through his steely gray eyes. "Fine," he said. But by the expression on his face, nothing was fine.

As Wallace served the appetizers, Mr. Larson summarized the daily mortgage and bond rates. Skye focused on her wretched salad on a stick and wished instead for the potatoes. For some reason Wallace did not return to the kitchen but stayed just out of reach behind Skye.

After another moment of financial details, Mr. Larson turned to Adelaide.

"And how was your day?" he asked.

Skye's mother set down her fork and sighed. She sat up straight and patted her loosely braided blond hair with her right hand.

186

"To tell you the truth, Arrowroot's success is almost doing me in!" she said with a laugh. "I can hardly keep enough stock on hand, and we're always short-staffed during the week."

Charles beamed at her. "The cost of doing business, I suppose. Perhaps you should consider hiring more staff."

"May I?" she asked with eagerness. "It would be so helpful."

"Of course!" Charles replied. "I think we've tested the waters long enough. Just make sure you have enough work for them all, and watch the overtime."

Adelaide laughed gently. "Of course, dear."

Charles turned his attention to his daughter.

"And now Skye?" he asked with a gleam in his eye. "Tell us about your day. Did everything go well with Dorran's departure?"

"So, you know about that," she replied calmly. She internally set up her guard and swallowed.

"Of course," he said, his face turning a shade darker. "After our conversations about you and the boy, it seems we are no longer able to trust you to yourselves." The man held up his hand as Skye leaned forward to reply. "Please do not interrupt. I do not think it is an exaggeration to say that we have been more than patient in this matter between you and the boy, Dorran. You've called him every night and I've said nothing, hoping that you would have sense enough to reduce your contact with him. You see him almost every day, either by bringing him food from Arrowroot, or you two going out together at the local coffee shop. But it has to stop. Now."

He paused as if waiting for her to reply, but she didn't. So Mr. Larson continued, his voice growing angry.

"Dorran is simply not conducive with this family, and I'll tell you why." He stared at her, as if waiting for a reaction that did not come. "First of all, his father is in prison for car theft. A 15-year sentence with nine years to go. Dorran's mother left after his incarceration. She had a long history of drug abuse, and is probably dead in some gutter, somewhere." The man leaned forward and glowered at Skye. "And this boy, Dorran? He helped his father steal cars! Served 18 months at Gilliam Youth Services Center in Denver! Brian and Lisa Parker took him in and helped him get back on his feet. But

188

that doesn't change the fact that he is still riff-raff! Think of how his influence could adversely impact our family! I will not let you bring in human garbage like that!"

The man paused, and looked at his wife, who remained expressionless. Then he continued his tirade.

"So until he is sent away to the army, your freedoms are restricted. If you need to work, Wallace will drive you. If you need to text, place a phone call, or receive one, someone will need to be with you. And while we're on that subject, please give Wallace your phone. Now."

Skye obediently pulled out her phone, turned it off, and handed it to Wallace, who watched her with keen interest.

"Adelaide," Charles said, looking to his wife. "You wish to say something?"

The woman's eyes watered, matching the sad smile on her face.

"Skye, dear, please understand that we are doing this only to look out for you. This Dorran, he is only using you to get to us. Surely you can see that. After he leaves, then things will settle back to normal. You'll see."

The pause was meant for her to interrupt, to blurt out, to argue or scream, but she did none of those things. Instead, with all the energy within her, she smiled.

"Father, Mother...I'm leaving," she said looking at both of them in turn.

Charles laughed. "Your school doesn't begin for at least another month," he said. "And remember our conversation about changing your major? I still think economics is your best choice."

Skye kept calm, though inside her heart was beating wildly. She took a deep breath.

"Father...Mother, you know I love you both. But I have to do what is best for me. I love Dorran. I plan to spend the rest of my life with him. And I understand what that means for this family." She shook her head. "I don't want your money. Give it to someone else." She looked at Wallace and then back at her dad. "It's time I learned to stand on my own two feet. I want to earn my way and make my own decisions. So I am leaving. Now."

"Leaving? Where will you go?" Charles bellowed, his voice turning angry.

Skye sighed and smiled again. "I'm all packed. I'll live with Liliane, finish school at Seattle University, major in advertising, and wait for Dorran to finish his training. Don't worry—you won't lose me. I'll come and visit. Promise!"

"Liliane?" Adelaide asked in a soft voice. "You've been talking with your sister?"

Skye turned around and looked at Wallace, then at her dad. "They never told you?" she asked, feeling a calm she never knew she had. "Maybe they missed those conversations, but yes. Liliane. My sister. Who is alive and doing very well."

"Miss Larson," Wallace began sharply. "You need to stop this. There is no way your father---"

"NO!" Adelaide shrieked, her face contorted and she rose to her feet. She grabbed glasses, dishes, silverware and threw them. She jerked the tablecloth and all its contents to the floor with a crash. Then she turned on her husband, her face pale, her voice shrieking.

"Charles! Charles I can't go through this again! I can't stand it here when Skye is at school! I've never gotten over losing Liliane—you know that! And if Skye leaves, I don't know what I will do!" She looked at Wallace, her eyes burning. "Get out! Get out of here! I don't want to see your face again!"

She grabbed Charles by his collar as if taken by a madness. "This is all your fault!

Your rules drove Liliane away and now you're doing the same with Skye! Fix it! Fix it now, or Skye won't be the only one leaving!"

As Wallace hurried from the dining room, Adelaide broke down in loud sobs, her body shaking. Finally, she walked out of the room, whimpering to her husband, telling him to fix the situation.

Charles' face went white. He stared at the floor with the broken glasses and plates.

Skye rose. "I should go," she said quietly. "When I get a new phone, I'll call you. I promise."

Her father's face filled with sudden terror.

"No, dear god, don't leave! Please wait!" He stood to his shaky feet. "I need to talk with your mother. Please don't go anywhere!" He stepped toward her, his face pleading. "Please...stay?" he asked, no longer the strong, in-control-CEO of Coeur d'Alene Bank & Trust. But now, a desperate father pleading with a strong daughter.

"All right," she said quietly. "I can wait until you get back."

As the man followed after his wife, the maids scrambled into the dining room, cleaning the mess. Skye watched as they quietly swept and mopped the floor and replaced the dining table cloth and all the table accessories, as if they had done this before. After the new plates were brought out, Skye picked the potato as an appetizer.

*

Twenty minutes later, Charles Larson returned, his face pale and his walk, shaky. Skye felt an impulse to run to him and hug him, but knew that would send the wrong message. So she remained in place, carefully chewing her Mongolian beef.

He sat in his seat, but did not touch the food in front of him.

"I've not seen your mother like that since before you were born," he said, taking a napkin and wiping his forehead. He stared at Skye, again apparently waiting for a reply that did not come. Skye simply stared at the table in front of her.

"Please don't leave right away," the man continued. "For your mother's sake."

"What about yours?" Skye asked, calm as before.

"Me?" the man asked with a laugh. "To be honest, sure, I'd miss you at mealtimes and seeing you round the house. But my life is still very full with all of my business activities. It consumes almost every waking minute." He shook his head. "But your mother. You two girls are her life, and it has been very hard."

Skye simply stared at him until their eyes met.

"I respect your decision," he said with a sorrowful expression. "You've grown up faster than I ever imagined. But it will be hard for you, you know."

Skye retained her composure. "I am not willing to sacrifice Dorran for a pile of money or businesses that consume my every waking minute."

The man looked lost in thought for several moments as the food continued to cool in front of him.

"Does Dorran feel the same way about you?" he finally said. "Now that you've thrown away your inheritance?"

Skye looked at her father, no longer concerned with hiding her feelings.

"I think so," she said. "But even if it ends up in flames, I know I can live on my own. You taught me that."

Chapter 18
Ice

Dorran sounded his feeble bike horn and squeezed his brakes simultaneously, his mind a flash of immobilization as his adrenaline kicked in. Fortunately, his speed was less than 35 MPH and the deer parted like the Red Sea: two darted one way and two ran the other. Dorran leaned his bike one way, then the next in a desperate attempt to avoid making contact. Unfortunately, his left shoulder bumped against the rump of one of the animals, sending him and his motorcycle zigging and zagging and sliding across a very wet and gravelly road. He lost balance and the bike fell sideways, taking him with it.

Everything happened so fast. Suddenly he was pinned on the ground, his left leg trapped beneath his bike. With a gasp, Dorran pushed upward with all of his energy, but his body and backpack were at the wrong angle and the bike wouldn't budge. He felt a sudden wet chill run along the outside of his left pant leg, and closed his eyes.

I just need a moment to rest.

*

The slamming of truck doors brought Dorran back to consciousness. Two pickups parked opposite where he lay, and three men and a boy ran to his side.

"Mister, are you okay? I was sure your number was up when I saw them deer cross." A tall man dressed in a flannel shirt and jeans was the first on the scene. Those who followed were likewise dressed.

As one they took the bike and carefully set it upright on its kickstand. The stocky man removed Dorran's backpack and helped him to his feet.

"Nice bike," another man said, walking around the motorcycle. "Besides a few dents and scrapes, it looks to still be in okay shape. I don't see any fluids leaking out."

The young boy hunched near Dorran and peered at his left leg. He grimaced as he looked back at the stocky man.

"Dad, I think he's all tore up!" he cried, his voice betraying his fears. "He's bleeding pretty bad."

"I'm okay," Dorran said placatingly. "It's nothing serious. I'll be all right." But even as he spoke, he felt light-headed. At the same time a sense of weariness came over him.

"You probably shouldn't be riding any more until you get yourself patched up," the stocky man said. "We can take you to a clinic. It ain't no trouble."

Dorran shook his head stubbornly. "That's okay. I just need a few bandages and I'll be fine."

"Where you headed?"

"Billings," Dorran replied.

"That's a few hours away still," said the third man, looking at the others. "He might be okay, and then again he might not." He looked at Dorran. "You might see more deer, too."

That was the last thing Dorran wanted to hear, knowing that another encounter might turn deadly.

The stocky man shook his head. "I don't feel right about you going on. Let us take you back to town. Can you afford a hotel?"

Dorran's energy level cratered, making it hard to even think. "A hotel sounds good," he agreed with a nod. "But there's no need for a ride. I can drive."

The man folded his arms. "Now what kind of Good Samaritans would we be if we just abandoned you like this? Those deer might just decide to take revenge and attack as soon as we leave."

Dorran laughed. "I don't want to put you to any trouble."

"Heck, it ain't no trouble," said the man. "We've been out getting wood until it started raining like mad. We came back early with only a partial load so there's plenty of room for your bike. My name's Jake, by the way." The man held out his hand.

"Dorran," he replied, taking it. "And I'll pay you for your trouble," he insisted.

The man hesitated, looking at Dorran's hand before letting go. "No need," Jake replied, as the two others rolled his bike across the road. "I got your pack. Now let's see if you can walk."

Dorran's left leg hurt and streamed blood as he started to hobble. He felt embarrassed by his weakness, but there was no time to think as stars filled his vision and he began to swoon. Jake caught him in time and helped him into the cab of his pickup.

Dorran buckled in, feeling his energy drain to even lower levels as Jake talked to his friends. He couldn't make out what was said, but there was an urgency in the man's voice. When he entered the truck, he took off down the road before his door was even closed.

"So, Dorran, where are you from?" he asked in a loud and tense voice.

But Dorran couldn't hear him.

*

A bed. Tubes, wires, an IV drip, and monitors that beeped. White drapes that hung along two sides of the room, and a clock on the wall that read 12:20 a.m. A sheet and blanket that covered his gown.

A gown?

Great, he thought. *A hospital room. Not a good sign.*

A nurse stood at the foot of his bed, looking at a clipboard and jotting down notes. She smiled when she saw him.

"How are you feeling?"

He took a quick inventory, his toes demanding most of his attention.

"My feet are freezing," he said in a morning, groggy sounding voice.

"I can fix that," she replied. In 30 seconds, she placed a warm blanket reaching from his knees to his toes.

"Thanks," he said, mind still fuzzy. "What happened?"

"You had a run-in with our local deer."

In a flash Dorran's memory returned: the darting animals, the swerving back and forth and his bleeding leg.

"On a motorcycle, no less," he said and sighed. He hoped his bike would still run after the accident. "Some guy named Jake brought me here. Have you seen him? I need to say my thanks."

The nurse smiled. "That guy Jake is my husband. You lucked out that they found you right away. We had to wrap your leg to stop the bleeding, but you probably won't need stitches. You lost some skin but you should be fine in a day or two."

Dorran's deadlines suddenly loomed in his head. "Great. So I can leave?"

"Not so fast." The woman said, taking a few steps toward him. "Let me find the doctor."

After a while an older woman with black hair entered the room, wearing a hospital badge and a purple smock.

"Dorran?" she asked. "I'm Doctor Jensen. You suffered bleeding and some skin loss from your accident. The wound isn't serious but you started going into shock. Are you certain you want to leave right away?"

"Shock? Did I lose a lot of blood?"

"No," she said, with a puzzled expression. "But you came in cold and clammy, and you slept for quite a while. Do you have any other conditions or recent injuries that could help us understand what may be happening?"

"No," Dorran said with a shake of his head. "I get ulcers sometimes, but I generally keep them under control."

"Well, I'd like to keep you through the night, just for observation," Dr. Jensen said. "And when you get back home, tell your doctor about your ulcers as soon as possible."

Dorran nodded his assent. After that the nurse asked him a lot of background health questions, and took his auto insurance information before he fell back asleep.

*

After a bland breakfast, Dorran checked out of the Bozeman Health Deaconess Hospital, though not as fast as he would like. He had to put up with his nurse wheeling him out to the parking lot. His motorcycle waited for him next to Jake's old beat up pickup, with its light blue peeling paint. Once the man got out, he handed Dorran his pack.

"You gave us a scare!" he said with a nervous laugh. "One minute you seemed fine, the next, not so much." Jake gave him a look. "How's the leg?"

"Better," Dorran said as he stepped away from the wheelchair and stretched. "Thank you, Jake." He offered his hand and the man grasped it firmly. "Much appreciated."

"That's what we do," Jake said with an obvious sigh of relief.

Dorran put his backpack and helmet on, started his bike, and slowly drove out of the parking lot. Just before he turned onto the main road, he noticed Jake and his wife, still watching him and waving. Dorran nodded and waved back.

After gassing up his motorcycle and grabbing a few snacks at a local Chevron station, he tested how his leg would fare for the day. His bandage felt thick and tight around his leg but it only slightly restricted his movement. The pain was minimal.

Dorran thought about Skye, how he should call her and let her know what happened. But he suspected she'd only worry. He determined to call her later that day, or maybe that night in Denver. But for now, he was three hours behind schedule and had time to make up.

Interstate 90 carried light-to-moderate traffic, and with its 75 MPH speed limit, the miles literally flew by. After Dorran made it to Billings, he walked around on his stiff leg and called Skye's number. But it went straight to voice mail so he explained briefly where he was, and that with any luck he would make it to Denver late that night and at *Tri Star* around 9 the next day.

After stopping every few hours to rest and eat, Dorran pulled into Denver that night around eight-thirty. By then he was exhausted and his leg hurt. After changing his bandage in the hotel, he snacked on a few more cupcakes from the Arrowroot Bakery. As he fell into a dead sleep, visions of kissing Skye carried him away.

Chapter 19
Fire

Adelaide Larson's small black suitcase lay open on a queen-sized bed, in one of the many posh bedrooms of the family estate. Her eyes narrowed as she examined a silky red shirt, one of Skye's favorites.

"I don't know if Liliane would like this," she worried out loud.

"Mom, whatever you bring will be fine. If you keep hesitating, your flight will leave without you."

Adelaide laughed, her eyes teary and her makeup beginning to run. "We have plenty of time. And it's been ever so long. I fear she won't want to see me once I get there."

Skye sighed but smiled. "Of course she wants to see you. She's probably as nervous as you, like both of you meeting for the first time."

Adelaide sighed heavily and wiped her eyes. "Except that I used to be her mother. Back then I should have stepped in and –"

"Mom," Skye said. She gently placed her hand on her mother's, and smiled. "It's all right. She told me she is excited to see you."

Adelaide gave her a look of disbelief. "She used those words?"

"The exact ones."

The woman looked at her daughter admiringly. "The way you stood up to your father last night...well, I just wanted to say how proud of you I am. I could never have handled it as well as you did. What is your secret?"

Skye placed two pair of nice stockings into the suitcase. "I guess I finally decided what I want, and was willing to lose everything to get it. And now," she continued with a genuine smile, "I have the freedom to be myself and not worry about every little thing I say to Dad. Or you."

The elder woman smiled as she selected a pair of slacks. "I've liked Dorran from that time I met him in the bakery. And I was amazed at his composure during the funeral when everyone thought he was Darrell's ghost!"

Skye reflected back to when she stood in front of a packed church of grieving people, reciting poems that gave the impression they were for her ex-boyfriend, when in reality they were meant for her and Dorran. He gave his confident support when she was beside herself with fear. She remembered sensing his care, which helped her focus and finish her speech.

"He was certainly braver than I would have been," Skye said.

"Didn't you say Dorran is on his way to Denver? Has he called you yet?"

Skye looked at her mom. "Wallace took my phone. Remember?"

"That *Wallace*." Her face colored as she stood. "We'll get you a new phone on the way to the airport today. And I have a couple of other errands, so we better hurry along."

*

Marcus seemed happier than normal as Skye and her mother approached the limo, each carrying a suitcase. He even gave them a pleasant smile while holding open the door and taking their luggage.

He tipped his hat. "Good morning, ladies!"

Adelaide tapped his shoulder in greeting as she passed by.

"Good morning, Marcus!" she said cheerfully. "Nice day for a drive, isn't it?"

"It certainly is, ma'am," he replied.

Skye peered at her mom as they took a seat. She waited until Marcus closed the door before speaking.

"What's that about?" she asked. "I've never heard you talk that nice to him."

Adelaide sighed. "Yes, well, when I think of how poor Marcus was demoted from butler and Wallace took his place, it seems to have a sense of unfairness about it. Don't you think?"

There was a twinkle in her eye that Skye recognized.

"You're plotting something." It wasn't a question.

Her mom held her purse between her hands and shrugged.

"I'm always plotting something. Haven't you learned that by now?"

Skye smiled slightly. "Typically you're not so flashy about it."

*

As the limousine neared the city of Spokane, Washington, Adelaide opened her large purse, rummaged around it and handed a thick padded envelope to Skye.

"First stop is a bank to which your father has no connections," she began. "He may disinherit you all he wants, but I certainly won't."

207

Skye froze. "What's this?"

"Something to start your new bank account. You will be the sole account owner, with no one else looking over your shoulder to see how you spend the money. It is yours, free and clear."

Skye looked at the envelope and frowned.

"He doesn't know about this."

Adelaide shook her head. "Though I wish he did. I'm tired of sneaking around hoarding money in different hiding spots." She looked Skye in the eye. "Did you know I overheard him on the phone the other day? I learned from that conversation the value of our family estate: over $500 million!" She fumed. "And *he* won't even give Liliane a dime. Not one single dime!"

"$500 million?" Skye's eyes widened as she handled the envelope.

Her mom laughed. "Don't worry, you only have a hundred thousand, my dear." She shook her head. "The same amount he pays that snake *Wallace* every year," she said, under her breath.

"That's too—" Skye began, but her mother put her hand on Skye's shoulder, shaking her head, her eyes glistening.

"No, no it isn't!" she said in a serious tone. "I have to do this. The guilt I feel for you and Liliane is piled so high it's choking me. Drowning me. And I cannot get rid of it, no matter how hard I try, how many therapy sessions I attend, or the charity events I host. It's still there, biting at me, nagging day after day." Her hands shook but there was a steady fire in her eyes. After a moment she settled back into normalcy. "There's an envelope with the same amount for Liliane. Just know that I will not let either of you suffer any more. Not if I can help it."

Skye stared at her, open mouthed, as if this person in front of her was a total stranger. All she ever remembered was her mother agreeing with what her father said.

Skye hugged Adelaide. "Thank you, Mom," she said quietly. "I mean it."

"I know you do. But I want you to promise me something."

"What is it?"

"Any time your balance drops below $10,000 you let me know. Until you are financially stable with a nice house, a good paying job, and everything else, I want to help out."

"Okay," Skye said softly. "But what about Father?"

Adelaide took a deep breath and smiled. "You should know that by law, half of what he owns is mine. So you are looking at a multi-millionaire."

"Wow, way to go Mom!" Skye said, beaming.

*

After setting up her bank account and buying the latest android phone, Skye and Adelaide reached the airport with plenty of time to spare. Skye called Dorran's number but it went to his voice mail. She figured they were probably playing phone tag, so she resolved to call again later.

Marcus said his good-byes with an agreed-upon return time, when Adelaide sat Skye down again.

"I want this weekend to be special," she said, pulling another envelope from her purse.

"Mom!" Skye began to protest, but her mother simply shook her head and made her take it.

"You have a motorcycle endorsement on your license, right?"

Skye nodded.

"All right then. You know what to do." She stood, hearing her flight number called, and hugged Skye tightly once more. "Have fun this weekend, okay?"

"Okay. Love you, Mom."

Adelaide let out a small sob. "Love you too, sweetie."

Chapter 20
Ice

Dorran's stomach hurt, and worse than normal. Whether from stress, lack of sleep or just plain ulcers, he did not know. He opened his tired eyes, grabbed his cell and checked to see if Skye called in the last couple of hours.

But there was nothing.

He worried something happened. She always answered his calls, or at least responded leaving by her own voicemail.

He flipped on the light switch in his sparsely furnished hotel room and looked at the blinking red numbers of the clock that read 7:01 a.m. He groaned, wishing it was later. Much later.

Tri-Star Rehabilitation Facility was Dorran's first stop but it didn't open until nine. After that he would go to Englewood Correctional Institute, where his dad was locked up. He was looking forward to that encounter even less than the one with Renée. He loved his sister of course, but drug addiction had torn his family apart since he was little, and now it showed its devastating impacts in her.

His dad, however, never seemed to improve himself in any meaningful way. Always the same complaining, feeling sorry for himself and casting doubts on Dorran's aspirations. Three of the reasons he limited his interactions to only once a year, and on Renée's birthday.

Dorran showered, rewrapped his leg with new bandages, and found some edible Continental Breakfast food in the tiny hotel lobby. The bananas, oatmeal and applesauce helped settle his stomach, making Dorran wonder if his pain came from his nerves. With a loaded plate in hand he returned to his room and watched part of a *Stranger Things* episode until it was time to leave.

Dorran limped slightly as he entered the Tri Star facility, holding a medium-sized package. The site was a complex of several separate buildings painting in varied shades of brown, with a large welcome sign in the middle, pointing to automatic glass double doors.

A middle-aged woman behind a carved wood counter smiled as he approached.

"Good morning," he said. "I'm here to see Renée Black. I called yesterday."

The woman glanced down briefly. "Yes, I see. Dorran?"

He nodded as she handed him a guestbook to sign. Then she pointed to her left while looking at a computer screen.

"She is in room 128 but not very active yet. I'll call ahead and let the nurse know you are coming. Give her a few minutes."

Dorran thanked her and slowly made his way down the expansive hallway, its walls filled with commercial inspirational artworks. He stopped in front of one made of a mature dandelion whose seeds drifted away into the blueness beyond. The caption beneath read:

Greatness: When we envision the extraordinary, we lay the foundation for our wildest dreams.

Dorran stood, frozen in place, wondering if he had pulled the plug on his greatness. Would the Army be able train him so he could start his own business? Or would he spend his time mainly repairing damaged trucks and Jeeps? So many things could have gone his way if he had only waited and not acted irrationally.

But it is only two years, four at most, he reasoned. But then would Skye still be there, waiting for him when he came back? He could not imagine life without her. But why wasn't she answering his messages? Did she change her mind about him while he was away? And Dorran wondered if he ever wanted come back to Coeur d'Alene. Wasn't that town simply holding him back from his dreams?

Someone rushed by, dressed in blue scrubs, but he hardly noticed. He refocused, folded those doubting thoughts away—far away, so that for now he wouldn't have to think about them. And he continued on.

Room 128 was located in one of the detached brown buildings, separated from the main office. He passed by other pictures, though none caught his attention as much as the dandelion.

He stood in front of a pastel-pink door and knocked quietly. The door opened and a smiling nurse in blue scrubs opened it.

"Your sister is ready to see you," she said cheerfully.

Dorran thanked her and walked inside. A couch across from a TV, a few well-placed chairs, a desk and a bed in the back corner greeted his eyes. And more inspirational pictures hung on the walls. But his eyes went right to his sister.

He took a few steps closer and stopped.

His sister?

He swallowed, placed the package carefully on the desk and forced himself to move closer.

This is not how he remembered her. She used to be perky, healthy, shining black hair, mischievous smile.

A few more steps, he told himself, *and you'll be there*. But he hated seeing her like this. Unkempt hair, pale face, hidden beneath several blankets, smile-less. But again, he pushed his fears and disappointment aside and walked up with a glowing smile.

She returned only a partial smile.

"Hey Monkey," he said.

"Hi Chief," she replied quietly.

They hugged and Dorran teared up at once.

"So, I heard you needed a little R & R," he said, trying to start out positive.

But Renée covered her face, the tears flowing.

"Oh god, I am so sorry Dorran!" She sobbed a while, him just holding her hand

and trying to keep his emotions under control. "I was stupid."

"Was it Richard?" he asked quietly.

She shook her head.

"Marjorie?"

Another shake, anger flaring.

"A boyfriend?"

"I wish," she said, wiping her eyes.

"Did you see Dad? Or hear from Mom?" he pressed, wanting to get to the reasoning.

Her anger seemed to get the best of her.

"It was you, butt-head!"

Dorran stepped back in shock. "Me?" he asked, pointing to himself, guilt beginning to creep in. "What did I do?"

Renée sobbed before regaining control of her voice. "So Lisa calls the other day, you know? Asks how I'm doing and all that. Then she says how proud of you she is now that your life is taking an adventurous turn. Yay! She says. You're in the Army where you can learn to run your own business someday." She sobbed louder than ever.

But Dorran didn't react. He stood there without saying a word.

"Why didn't you call me up and tell *me*?" she roared.

"I was going to when I came to visit."

"Oh, that's real convenient," she said. She sat up and glared. "Did you know that I was counting the days until I could get out of this hole? One more year of school then I could move."

It was then that Dorran started to connect the dots.

"To Coeur d'Alene," he said quietly.

"Bingo!" she yelled. "I can't stand being here alone anymore! No one at school likes me, my teachers all suck and now...this." Her voice died to a whimper.

Dorran took her hand and held it, even though she tried to pull it back. "I am sorry," he returned quietly. "I didn't know."

"I know that," Renée sniffed. "You've got your great job and friends and now a *girlfriend*," she said. "And I have to learn this from Lisa?"

"Okay, okay," he soothed. "Things just happened really fast and I got caught up in it. What do you want to know?"

She gave him a look.

"Is she really a millionaire's daughter?"

Dorran nodded.

"And you like her?"

Another nod.

"Does she even know about me?"

Dorran smiled. "After I told her what happened, she wanted to fly down the same day. She also has a sister."

Renée looked thoughtful and sat up. "I think I like her."

"I think I love her."

"Okay then, tell me *everything*."

Dorran started from the beginning when they clashed, the fire drill adventure, the water skiing and up to the present.

"But she's not answering my phone," he worried out loud.

Renée snapped her fingers three times. "Hey Chief! You know how many times I broke or drowned my phone? More times than I can count. Give her a break already! I'm sure something happened to it!"

Dorran sighed, his tension easing. "You're right."

"I'm always right."

"Uh-huh."

They looked into each other's eyes.

"I *am* sorry," Dorran said.

"Me too," Renée replied. "But never again, okay? Tell me this stuff before I hear it second-hand and have another nervous breakdown."

Dorran looked at her. "And you lay off the hard stuff."

Her face colored. "I know. And now I have to take these other stupid meds 'cause they think I'm addicted to opioids. It REALLY sucks!"

"You'll be out in no time," Dorran said. He took his package from the table. "Here, I got you something." He handed it over to her. "Happy birthday."

Renée tore the brown wrapping to shreds like she normally did, causing Dorran to laugh. She held up the box and read aloud.

"3-D Wooden Locomotive Puzzle Construction Kit. How many parts?"

"Only 443 and it should take you about nine to sixteen hours." Dorran grinned. "But it will move by itself when it's done."

"You turd."

"Now *that's* the Monkey I know."

*

Dorran rode his '69 Honda CB750 ten miles southwest of Denver to reach Englewood Correctional Institution. He used the time to process his sister's struggles, fight off the guilt for not talking to her about his plans, and list the things he would say to his dad when he got there. He promised himself he would do everything he could to get her out of Denver come next

June. Lisa and Brian would likely take her in. One phone call would do it.

The flat landscape was colored mostly brown, with a few hills in the distance, nothing like Idaho. Dorran found himself missing those green forested lands. He couldn't wait to get back home.

The prison building rose to three levels, light beige all around, and secured by a high-wire fence. There was no traffic, and a guard appeared by the gate entrance. He stood tall and menacing, holding out his hand for Dorran to stop at the gate.

"What can I do for you?" the guard said as soon as Dorran switched off the bike. The man lacked a friendly tone.

"I've come to visit my father," Dorran replied. He eyed the vacant visitor parking lot. "Did something happen?" he asked, partly looking for an excuse to skip the prison visit entirely.

The guard looked at him. "We're under a lockdown."

Dorran smiled inside. "I see," he said. "Well, thanks anyway."

He started to turn his bike around when the guard held out his hand. "Can I see some identification?"

Dorran looked at him, thinking he probably still needed a record of every visitor who came on site. But he held up his hands in a friendly gesture.

"It's okay. I'll come back another time."

But the man was insistent. "Identification, please."

Dorran knew the guard had no right to demand anything of him, especially since he was not yet actually on the prison property. His stomach hurt and he didn't feel like complying. He shook his head and started his Honda.

But the guard stepped forward and turned the bike off.

"Hey!" Dorran said, his anger rising. "What are you doing?"

The guard stepped back, his face softening slightly.

"We are asking all visitors to help with our current ...situation."

"Situation?"

The man nodded.

"We have reason to believe that certain individuals may be targeted by prisoners, or their contacts on the outside. We need to convey that information to them so they do not come to any future harm."

"Huh," Dorran said, not sure he believed the guard.

"Well, my name is Dorran Black and I came to see my father, Larry Black. I live two states away so I doubt I'm in any danger."

"Thank you for that information," the guard said, his interest piqued. "Now if I can please see your identification."

Dorran sighed, still not wanting to comply. He just wanted to go home. But he didn't want to create a scene, either. And what if this Federal institution was to inform his Army superiors of this incident? It could definitely make things hard at boot camp.

Finally he stood, opened his wallet and pulled out his Idaho driver license. The guard looked it over and nodded.

"Just a moment," he said, walking over to a booth just inside the gate and placing a call. In a moment the guard opened the gate and returned Dorran's license. "Please park in the designated area for motorcycles. Our warden will meet you there."

Dorran stared at him, his heart racing. He shook his head. "I don't think so."

The guard took two steps forward, blocking Dorran's ability to move his bike anywhere.

"Mr. Black, let me assure you that you are not in any danger. The warden simply wants to speak to you and ask you a few questions."

"And my father?"

The man shrugged. "That would be up to the warden. Your help in this matter is appreciated."

Dorran felt a lump in his stomach. He must be the one they were looking for. Did some prisoners threaten to hurt him if his dad didn't comply with their demands? Was there a contract out on him, even now? He swallowed as he looked around the premises.

"Okay, fine," he said in a low voice.

The guard stepped back and Dorran drove through. He found the bike parking area easily enough. That was where three men were standing in the middle of an empty parking lot. Two guards and apparently the warden himself, wearing a dark suit and red tie. He was a short, balding man, who held a handkerchief to his head.

"Leave your backpack and any cell phones or electronic devices with me," the taller guard said, stepping forward.

Dorran nodded and complied. After setting his pack down and handing over his cell phone, the guards frisked him quickly but gently, though he flinched when they touched his left leg.

"He's clean," the taller guard spoke to the warden.

The old man stepped forward.

"Dorran Black, my name is Warden Johnson. You seem to be our missing link!" He offered his hand and Dorran took it.

"Mr. Johnson, I'm afraid I don't understand what is happening here," Dorran replied.

"Please come inside," the man invited with a kind smile. "So we can get this all sorted out and resume our normal schedule."

Dorran's feet felt like lead. Past images of prison doors flooded his memory as he slowly walked toward the building. Were they going to arrest him? Did his father do something to implicate him in a crime? Did someone really threaten his life?

As Dorran stepped inside the entrance, he saw the shattered remains of the food service dining room. Most of the glass was swept into piles, as were the broken tables, chairs and plates. But he was ushered the other way through a long hall, upstairs and finally into the Warden's plain office. The older man sat at an old wooden desk after dismissing the guards. Dorran sat on the other side.

The Warden looked at Dorran and smiled.

"I take it by the look on your face that you haven't seen the local news."

Dorran shook his head.

"I thought not. Okay, let me fill you in. Yesterday, Larry Black started a riot in the food service dining room. He had a lot of backing and one of our guards ended up in the hospital. It took three hours before we were able to control the situation but by that time—" he waved his hand "—well, you saw the damage."

Dorran processed what he heard, more disgusted than ever by his father. What an embarrassment.

"I still don't understand," he finally said. "What does this have to do with me, except that I'm his son?"

The man's face lit up. "Ah yes, now this is the interesting part. Around three yesterday afternoon he started demanding to know where you were. I guess you were expected to visit him because he claimed that we were holding you against your will. And from looking at our visitor records in the past, you've come on July 24th every year for the past three years."

Dorran nodded.

"I'm curious. Why on that date, Dorran?"

"I come down each year to see my sister Renée on her birthday. On my way back home, I stop by and visit my dad."

Understanding and satisfaction came over the man's face. Then his eyes narrowed. "But this year you came late? Why is that?"

Dorran scratched his neck. "On the way down here I hit a deer and was hospitalized," he explained. "You might have noticed my limp."

Warden Johnson nodded. "I did." He folded his hands in front of his face as if to consider how much he should say. He paused a full minute before continuing.

"Your father thought we were holding you, and that's why he became violent."

Dorran laughed. "I have a hard time believing he ever cared for me *that* much."

"No, I suppose not, but you were part of his plan to escape. A very important part." The man opened a drawer and pulled out a crude makeshift knife, about a foot long. "And he was wielding this."

Dorran shrugged, more confused than ever.

The man lay back in his chair. "We interviewed every inmate and got a few to snitch. Apparently, your father was counting on your visit to plan his escape."

"What?! I would never help him escape!" Dorran's face turned hot.

"That's not what I mean," the Warden said, holding up his hands. "From what I understand he was going to take you as his hostage. In fact, he was going to stab you in the stomach with that knife," he said, pointing at the blunt object. "Let you bleed out a bit. Then claim you have some sort of intestinal disorder and demand that both of you be released before you died."

Dorran's mouth fell open. "I have ulcers," he finally said quietly.

"We've noticed Larry becoming more erratic as time goes by. We've had to discipline him and until recently he always came back around."

The warden paused again, allowing Dorran to process the information.

"That SOB," Dorran muttered, his anger peaking.

"I agree with that assessment," the warden said. "He's been moved and will likely be incarcerated at the Supermax prison in Florence. He's looking at another

20 years." He paused and sighed. "If I may offer a piece of advice?"

Dorran nodded eagerly. "Of course."

"If I were you, I'd think twice before visiting him ever again."

"Advice accepted," Dorran replied, his mind entrenched in darkness. He could have been killed if he showed up here yesterday. And what would have become of his dreams then? What would Skye have done?

"Well, I think that clears things up," the man said happily. "Thank you Dorran, for your time. I'm sorry this had to happen, you coming all the way and all." He extended his hand. "The guards will escort you out."

Dorran froze, a thought hitting him fully. Something that haunted him since he was 15 years old, a bunch of doubt mixed with fear. He simply stayed in place and looked the man in the eye.

"Warden Johnson, I have helped you with your investigation," he said calmly and slowly. "I was wondering if you could return the favor."

The man withdrew his hand and his smile faded.

"If I can," he replied. "What do you need?"

Dorran's eyes watered slightly and his heart felt heavy.

"Do you know what happened to my mother? Do you know where she is?"

Warden Johnson's face clouded over, a pensive look replacing the former relaxed expression. Again, he clasped his hands in front of his face, as if considering how much, if anything, he should say.

"Yes, I do," he said sadly. "But I don't think you want to hear it."

Dorran swallowed. "I would like to lay the question that I've asked myself many times over the last six years, to rest," he said. "I often wonder if I came back to Denver if I would someday find her. That could be a reason for an eventual return."

The warden's face turned serious. "Very well. As I understand it, your father was relying on your mother's testimony as an alibi when he initially went to court. He claimed she would be able to prove his innocence." He cleared his throat. "But she never showed up."

Dorran nodded. "She wasn't at my hearing, either."

The man nodded in understanding. "Yes, I know. The story goes that after your father was sentenced, he had one of his friends on the outside offer her some bad drugs, which she readily took." Mr. Johnson shook his head sadly. "She was the Jane Doe that was reported as deceased the next day."

"Are you certain?"

He nodded slowly. "The DNA matched."

His mom murdered? And by his dad? Dorran could remember them fighting from time to time, but never in his wildest dreams did he imagine this as a possibility. He had figured she shacked up with some bum around town and was probably still a user.

But murdered? As a Jane Doe?

The floodgates opened and Dorran could not stop them. The warden offered him a new handkerchief, which Dorran accepted. A few minutes passed with him releasing his emotions and the warden looking away, valuing his privacy to mourn.

Finally, Dorran stood. "Thank you, sir," he said. And offered his hand.

The man stood and took it. "I think you've turned out pretty well despite the circumstances," he said warmly. "An excellent reputation as a mechanic, a wealthy girlfriend, and a promising career in the Army." He nodded. "I wish you the best of luck, son."

"You don't miss a thing," Dorran said.

"I'm paid not to," he returned with a smile. His phone rang just then and he answered it, spoke a thank you, and hung back up. "And speaking of girlfriends, you have a visitor at the front gate."

Chapter 21
Fire

Skye sat waiting for Dorran on her brand-new red Harley Sport Glide. She grinned as he passed through the gate and stopped next to her. He popped out his kickstand and pulled off his helmet, but his face was not that of surprised wonder like she had imagined. It was full of anguish, pain, misery.

But he met her and they hugged a very long time. He pulled her in close to him and did not let her go. She did the same, which restricted part of her breathing. Then he kissed her repeatedly and hugged her again.

Dorran said nothing during that entire time, causing Skye to wonder and worry. Finally, he pulled away and choked out one word.

"Hungry?"

*

Skye felt shaky as she sat beside Dorran, beneath the outside huge umbrellas at The Melting Pot restaurant in Littleton. Something was wrong, that was clear, but what? After he ordered milk and she a hot tea, his body seemed to relax. But he held his stomach with his right hand.

"Ulcers?" she asked quietly.

He nodded and looked at her. "Thanks for coming. Where'd you get that awesome bike?"

Skye shook her head. "No way. You first. What is going on?"

He blinked and turned serious. "Too many things. My sister Renée overdosed after Lisa told her what I didn't—that I joined the military, not knowing she was counting the days until her graduation next year when she could move up to Coeur d'Alene."

"Oh, Dorran!" she said, paling.

The waiter set the drinks down on the table and left.

But Dorran continued. "My father started a riot in the prison yesterday when I didn't show up. He wanted to use me as a hostage and knife me so they would let both of us go. That was his escape plan! One guard was hospitalized. They moved my dad

234

somewhere else, and now he'll likely get another 20 years."

Skye was shocked. "Dorran, no!"

Now his face filled with tears. "Oh, and there's more," he said slowly. "After he was sent to prison, my father ordered a hit on my mother. She died of a drug overdose the next day."

Skye blinked, looked away, and blinked again.

"And to think I thought I had family problems," she whispered.

"I wouldn't blame you if you wanted out of this relationship," Dorran said. "My family is no good."

Skye narrowed her eyes. "Talk about family dysfunction? My father and I had a *disagreement* Thursday night."

"Uh-oh."

"Yeah, it didn't go well. I ended up telling him I didn't want his money. But at least I don't have to worry about spies peeking around every corner."

Dorran's cold hand took hers and she squeezed.

"I'm sorry," he said gently. "You gave up a lot for me."

"I'm not sorry," she replied with a slight laugh. "And I didn't give it up for anyone but myself. And actually, it's a relief. But that is why you weren't able to reach me. Wallace took my phone."

Dorran's face turned dark.

"He. Took. Your. Phone?"

She held up her new one and nodded. "So Mom got me this. You probably thought my calls were spam." She smiled as Dorran checked his own cell.

He rolled his eyes. "Yep. There you are. And four voicemails. Sorry!"

"Don't be. You had enough on your plate."

"So what are you going to do?"

"Hold on there, slick," she said. "I'm not through with you yet. You haven't told me why you didn't show up yesterday as planned."

Dorran told her about the deer, and left nothing out. Skye felt tension mount inside as he spoke, becoming almost unbearable as he finished.

"I bought some camping gear in case you want to sleep under the stars," she said quietly. "But we probably need to fly you home so you can see a doctor."

Dorran threw her a careless glance. "I've survived this long. A few more days won't matter. Anyway, I actually love camping.

Though I am getting tired. Not sure how much energy I have left."

"Leave that to me," Skye said. "I've been checking some places out."

*

St. Vrain State Park was an easy 30-minute drive north of Denver. A quick reservation call gave Skye several camping options. As they entered they saw a number of families with pitched tents and RV's, but Skye and Dorran picked a site away from most of the campers and close to one of the ponds.

Dorran seemed pleased with the arrangements and went right to work putting both tents up. Together they watched the golden sunset reflect against the nearby water, and Skye couldn't help feel that they dodged a bullet. By a single day. What could have happened scared her, and she fought her fear, trying to push it out of her mind.

Clouds moved in, masking the sunset as Dorran built a fire in the pit. Skye moved to one of the two supersized lounge chairs nearby and he joined her, wrapping his arms around her and squeezing gently.

"That feels good," she said. "It's been a long time."

Dorran stopped squeezing. "What do you mean?"

She wriggled around and faced him. "You know, you're the first guy out of five I've dated who hasn't tried to jump my bones?"

Dorran laughed. "What? Serious?"

She nodded. "My father took it upon himself to handpick these *gentlemen*, as he called them. Of course they were all sons of my dad's business partners, all hornier than a ten-peckered toad."

Dorran laughed at that. "Sons of something else I'd say."

Skye's eyes narrowed. "What really got me was that my father didn't care. 'Boys will be boys and all that,' he always said. Only once did he step in."

"Oh? When was that?"

"When a guy named Warren snuck into our house. He tried to find my room, but he found my mother in hers instead."

"Oops," Dorran said.

"Oh yeah, and he was *buck-naked*."

She watched his eyebrows rise, a deep smile beginning to form.

Skye laughed aloud. "My mother was so funny."

"What did she do?"

238

"She put her hands on her hips and said, 'Well, honey, you do look ripe for the picking but my husband will be here any minute. So we'd better get to it.' Warren lost it and ran out of the house yelling, and still naked. We never heard from him after that." Skye sighed sadly. "And then there was Darrell."

"Ah yes, Darrell. You also called him a pervert."

She nodded. "That's being overly nice." She felt anger mount. "So get this: the day I get out of school for the summer, he wants to go out. I say fine and we're driving to a party of some friends." She swallowed and continued. "He unbuckles his seat belt and attacks me, wanting to do it right then and there." She felt Dorran squeeze her gently again, making her feel absolutely safe. "I lost control of the car while trying to slap him away or knee him in the groin. That's when I swerved into the wrong lane, swerved out of that lane, off the road and into the air. That car must have flipped and rolled four times."

"I believe it," Dorran said quietly, holding her firmly.

Skye sighed deeply. "Whew, that's the first time I told anyone the whole story." She paused for a moment. "So what made you different from them?"

Dorran sighed and she felt him shudder. "To understand that, I'd have to go back and tell you about *my* past."

"I'm all ears," she said hopefully.

Chapter 22
Ice

Dorran hesitated, his doubts nagging at him. He knew that once he started telling his story, there was no going back. Everything would be laid bare, the things he never wanted anyone else to know. Part of him wanted to change the subject entirely, afraid of Skye's reaction after she learned about his past. Especially after what she learned about his father starting a prison riot. He could imagine the social media headlines: *Multimillionaire's daughter teams up with son of notorious jailbird.*

But another part of him knew this was the acid test. Would she reject him, or accept him?

"You don't have to explain yourself," Skye said, pulling Dorran's thoughts to the present. "I can simply envision you as one schooled properly in the art of manners."

Dorran laughed, feeling his face heat up. "Hardly." He cleared his throat. "Okay, so here goes: I helped my dad steal cars in

Denver from age ten to fifteen. Five years of juvenile delinquency."

"You started young."

Dorran grunted. "I was small and could fit into tight spaces."

"So, did you still go to school? Or was this a night job?"

"Oh yes, school was a must. Some nights we worked but it was mostly weekends. I thought we were just on a fun adventure at first, trying to hide from people and sneak around. Dad would say the cars belonged to this friend or a company who hired him to transport them."

Skye nodded. "When did you learn how to fix them?"

Dorran shrugged. "I was always fascinated with how they were put together, and how I would cherry them out if I had the chance. But at the time we only stole and sold them to support my family—mainly their drug habits, of course. I learned on-the-job fixing with Max and a lot of self-study."

He paused, waiting for a response. A rebuke. A judgmental expression of any kind. But she said nothing. Did nothing. Her face revealed nothing.

"Just before we were arrested, Finn told me the police were watching us," he continued.

Skye's eyes lit up. "How did he know?" she asked.

"Maybe he or his parents saw them, I don't know. But I didn't say anything to Dad."

"Why not?"

"He would have told me to shut up and mind my own business, or claim I was lazy and wanted to get out of the work. That was his style. If my stomach was hurting, or I was tired, or feeling sick. He'd always say the same thing.

"Finally, one night we were caught in a raid and I was whisked off to juvey. Sentenced to 18 months with help from a crappy lawyer. There in that wonderful institution, I had a tiny room, a single blanket and an old bed that creaked."

Skye stirred but it seemed more like a shiver.

"No one came to visit me. Mom disappeared. I knew Dad couldn't see me, but my uncle and aunt stayed away on purpose. Not even a phone call. They always liked Renée, and they wouldn't let her come by either. No grandparents.

"So I was lonely without any friends. I never ate or slept much. But after a few months, one night everything changed." He waited, realizing he was about to reveal something he never told anyone. Something so personal he knew that it might blow up his relationship with Skye. And if that happened, she would be gone forever. But if she stayed, it was meant to be.

"What happened?" she asked, interrupting his thoughts.

He paused even longer, still unsure. But he finally decided to let his impulse of trust call it.

"One night a female guard—I don't want to say her name—came in to check on me. She was early twenties and cute. I'd seen her around but didn't think she noticed me. She found me shivering in my bed with only one blanket and seemed to feel sorry for me. Brought me a couple more blankets and a thick bed spread, probably out of her own pocket. She asked about my mattress laying there in the middle of the floor. I explained that the frame squeaked so much I couldn't sleep. And from that night on she became my *friend*."

"At least you had someone."

Dorran laughed, feeling his face heat up yet again. "Yeah...well, it soon went way beyond the normal limits of what I would call an appropriate relationship."

"Oh." Skye bit her lip.

"Oh yeah, and to the point where I looked forward to her visits every night, even going to bed before everyone else. We were...intimate."

Skye simply nodded slowly, indicating her understanding.

"So, did you finally break it off?"

Dorran shook his head, feeling all the disappointed and hurt emotions rushing back. "I never would have left her. I thought I loved her and she loved me. But she was found out by the higher ups, or someone squealed. And from what I understand, I wasn't the only buddy she had. In fact, several other female guards had their own personal favorites. They covered for each other for quite a while before everything blew up and a lot of people lost their jobs. Then one night she didn't come into my room, though someone else did."

"Who?"

"Brian Parker. He worked part time at the detention center and I think he was trying to keep an eye on me."

"Why was he in your room?"

"He came to tell me what he learned about the guard. But I was ready for *her*. And I mean *ready*. Brian knocked on the door and I opened it, buck naked."

Skye's body shook with laughter and soon Dorran joined her.

"Yeah, but not so funny then," he continued. "Anyway, after letting me get dressed, he said he had some bad news. That guard had been fired the night before. Apparently, they threatened her with a warrant of arrest. So, she went home, overdosed on opioids, and died."

"Oh no, Dorran!"

He nodded. "I was a wreck. Cried every night. Stayed in my room most of the time. Returned to my routine of hardly eating anything and not sleeping. And soon I was nothing but skin and bones, which I hid until my physical. They looked at me and estimated I lost about 20 pounds. From there they put me into a hospital, but at least there I was looked after and had all the TV I wanted. I could even control the remote.

"Because Brian and Lisa weren't family, they had to go through a lot to get visitation privileges. Even a hearing before a judge."

"A hearing? Just to visit?" Skye looked incredulous.

Dorran nodded. "A formality. But the reasoning was fairly one-sided. After they explained that my parents were gone and my uncle and aunt refused to visit, there was no one. They presented the stats for kids who went through juvenile like that, and provided my latest medical results. I think it scared the judge. He gave them permission to visit anytime, 24/7, especially since they both worked in the medical field and had prior experience with juveys like me." He sighed and a small smile formed. "They literally saved my life, visiting daily, and sometimes staying for a few hours while we played games.

"So my mom abandoned me when I needed her most. The guard who I thought I loved committed suicide. That taught me to keep to myself, because if I didn't, the very same thing was sure to happen again. Like a bad karma never ending. So yes, it is out of respect for you that I haven't jumped your bones, but mostly to keep me from getting hurt."

Skye wiped at her eye and smiled. "Hard lesson to learn," she said, pressing closer.

"Just so you know, I'm not one to abandon others, and I'm not going to start with you."

Dorran's eyes watered as his built-up fears and angst suddenly melted away. He sighed. "Thank you, though that was a different reaction than what I expected."

She looked at him and frowned. "Why is that?"

"After everyone at juvey learned what happened, I was blackballed. No one would talk to this white trash boy, and that included all the kids and adults. I just figured I would always be an outcast."

"You are not white trash," Skye said defiantly.

Dorran chuckled. "I was growing up. I didn't know any different and the kids in juvey weren't any better."

Skye wrapped her arms around his. "That doesn't matter to me. It never has." She paused. "So, I take that to mean you haven't been intimate for six years?"

"I haven't even gone out with anyone for six years," he said. "You're the first real girlfriend I've ever had."

Skye hugged him.

Dorran set his jaw. "And call me old fashioned, but after everything I've been through, there has to be a strong commitment before that intimacy is justified in my mind."

"You mean marriage?" she asked.

Dorran grinned. "Are you proposing?"

Skye smiled. "Not yet. But honestly, what you just said is a relief. I was burned out on guys who wanted to always get in bed from day one and mate like rabbits." She sighed deeply. "So, what's your schedule like at boot camp?"

The sudden change in topic created a palpable feeling in the air. From peaceful and calm to stressful, ominous.

"It's ten weeks long," Dorran replied, keeping his feelings wrapped tightly. "They take my cell phone and other personal stuff, but I can write to you, and I will. We'll go through three different phases—red, white, and blue—each emphasizing different parts of everything military. We graduate week ten with a ceremony."

"Am I invited?"

"Of course! I'll be expecting you."

"And after graduation?"

"They call it AIT, for Advanced Individual Training, where I'll start individualized instruction. So with any luck, I'll begin formal mechanics training."

"And you are there for two years?"

Dorran nodded. "They agreed on two years active service followed by two years inactive duty. But hopefully after those two years I'll have the training I need to start my own business. By then you'll graduate from Seattle and we can be together."

"I can't wait," she said.

*

"Ready?" Dorran asked, as he slid his helmet over his head.

Skye nodded and gave the thumbs-up sign as Dorran started his bike. It was early morning on July 26, with plenty of sunlight available for the next 13 hours, when they would cover most of the distance back home. Dorran's stomach hurt for most of the day but he didn't mind. Having Skye beside him more than made up for any pain he felt. He treasured every minute with her, every stop, every passionate kiss or hand holding or conversation they shared. Precious moments he would remember at boot camp in Fort Jackson, South Carolina, when she wasn't there. He wished he could freeze time, so he would not have to be away from her, but it seemed as if the day simply flew by. And before he knew it, the sun was setting and they camped for the night, about four hours from Coeur d'Alene.

The hardest part of the next day was that last hug with Skye. He wanted to hold her forever but finally, Skye stepped back, turned quickly and rode away on her bike. She didn't say a word. Or perhaps she couldn't.

The next few days were little more than a blur, with friends checking in on him, wishing him well, buying him beers at the pub, trying to convince him to move to Canada and elope. At times running away seemed tempting but Dorran knew he would regret that decision for the rest of his life. Besides, he wasn't about to walk away from something he committed to, be that a job or a long-distance relationship. One way or another he knew it would work out. It had to.

*

Knock knock.

Dorran opened the downstairs door to his upstairs apartment. As he had hoped, Finn, Max, and Trey stood there, waiting to give him a final send off.

"Come on up," Dorran invited. His pace slackened, though, as he made his way up the stairs. His increasing stomach pains almost stopped him mid-stride.

"You okay?" Finn asked good naturedly, as they entered the after-party apartment with its trashcans overflowing with beer bottles, used paper plates and pizza boxes with leftovers inside. "Or just getting old?"

Dorran shrugged. "This is me on three hours of sleep."

Trey surveyed a few gifts lying on the black card table, and picked up a personalized compass given by Max. By now Dorran had memorized the words:

Go confidently in the direction of your dreams and live the life you imagined!

Inspiring as the words sounded, he found it difficult to be enthused by them. His heart was here, now. Not anywhere else. But he couldn't stop time or turn it backward, wish as he might.

Trey laughed as he picked up a coffee mug with the words, *Good luck finding better coworkers than us!*

"It was a fun party last night," Finn said cheerfully.

Trey chuckled. "Yeah, you and Sage Rollins got pretty cozy. What's with that?"

Finn's face flushed a little and he grinned. "Guess we'll see."

"Olivia Anderson was looking you over more than once," Dorran said. "Or didn't you notice?"

Trey's face went red. "I noticed. And we talked. A little. But mostly about your up-and-coming boot camp adventures. I think Skye put her up to it."

Dorran snorted. "Wouldn't put it past her." He looked around at the half-messy apartment, eying the black helium balloons and their various slogans: *You're Dead to Us; We will miss you for 5 minutes; We were just starting to like you; Hope You Fail;* and, *Leaving? We didn't know you had started.* His favorite was the gold banner along the back wall with the words, *Later Traitor.*

"All packed?" Max asked.

"Just a small duffel bag. They don't allow us to hold on to a lot of personal items at boot camp, so I figured I'd keep them here."

Trey nodded. "Smart move."

Dorran looked over at Max.

"Skye hired some folks to clean up and pack the rest of my stuff," he continued. "Should be here tomorrow."

Max shrugged and nodded. "No rush. It's all good."

"Any word on my replacement?"

Max stuffed his hands into his pockets. "Not yet, but I've had a few calls. You know how it is. Just takes time."

A *reveille* ringtone sounded and Trey pulled out his phone and stepped away. A moment later he returned.

"Sorry Dorran, duty calls," he said, his face filled with disappointment. "Good luck in basic training!"

They shook hands and traded pats on the back.

"Thanks for coming," Dorran said.

"Wouldn't miss your last day!" Trey said with a grin. "Now get out there and make something of yourself, all right?"

Dorran laughed and nodded. "Okay."

Another knock sounded on the door below.

"I'll get that!" Trey shouted as he headed downstairs. "Pretty sure I know who it is!" In a moment, Skye appeared, carrying a few large boxes marked *Alpine Bakery*. She set them on the table, said hi to Max and Finn, and turned to Dorran.

"Ready for breakfast? My treat!" she offered expectantly. "And I'll even drive."

"Sure," Dorran replied. "Can't pass up an offer like that, but let me get ready. Max, Finn, I'll see you guys later before I leave."

They nodded and headed out the door as Dorran went straight to his bathroom. After finishing, he threw some cold water on his face before grabbing a wrapped package on his card table.

Has to be my nerves, he thought to himself. *That's all it is.* His stomach now hurt worse than it had in a long time, though he was sure last night's pizza and beer didn't help. But he determined to endure it until he was at boot camp where a doctor could check him over and help fix the ulcers.

*

As Skye drove her BMW along the city streets, Dorran's stomach pains seemed to subside. He wanted to enjoy every last second with Skye, and remember everything about this day. He knew it would be what carried him through the next couple of hard years. *It's just bittersweet*, he told himself repeatedly. *To get what you want, this has to happen. And in the end it will be worth it.*

As they left the city and drove through rural neighborhoods that Dorran didn't recognize, he turned to her.

"I take it we're not eating at Calypsos."

Skye simply shook her head. "Relax, it's a surprise. I think you'll like it."

He reached for her hand and she held his for a few seconds before returning back to the wheel. After a few more miles the road turned private and Skye drove through a fancy gate, slowly making her way past acres of manicured lawn and finally a huge mansion.

Dorran's stomach pain flared.

"Not sure this is a great idea," he said quietly. "Remember my call with Wallace?"

Skye parked the car, unbuckled, leaned over and kissed Dorran.

"Wallace has been reassigned to other duties by the Larson Estate. You won't be seeing him."

Dorran's eyebrows shot up. "Is that so?"

Skye's face glowed. "It is. In fact, there have been a number of changes in our family over the past several days. Some you already know about."

Dorran hesitated, his hopes building. "And do these changes affect...us?"

Skye nodded. "They are mostly about us, but also about Liliane."

"Your sister?"

"Mother gave my father an ultimatum: either he accepts me and Liliane as we are and provides for us equally. Or, she leaves him, takes half the Larson Estate, and splits it equally between the three of us."

"I caused this," Dorran said, guilt mounting.

Skye laughed. "Not even," she countered. "This has been building in my mother ever since Liliane left. She's been a dormant volcano until now. Father's response to you and me was the last straw."

"So, he still doesn't accept me," Dorran said. "But he'll will tolerate me because of her threat?"

Skye nodded. "For now. But that might change and he could learn to accept you. Or not. To me it doesn't matter." She took his hand, her eyes brimming. "Dorran Black, you are mine no matter what happens."

Dorran couldn't speak for the intense warmth that passed from his chest and moved into his throat. But he pulled her hand toward himself and kissed it, and hugged her tightly. Then he handed her the package.

She quickly unwrapped it—a plaque with a picture of both of them together. The engraving below read *I love you more than the miles between us*.

Skye wiped her eyes as she handed him a small wrapped box. Inside was a 14k yellow gold link bracelet.

No words interrupted them. Just more tears, hugs and many passionate kisses.

The elderly Marcus met them at the entrance door. He looked immeasurably happy as Skye stepped between him and Dorran.

"Dorran, meet Marcus, our newly re-established butler of the Larson Estate."

Dorran grinned and shook the man's hand firmly.

"Congratulations!" he said.

"Thank you, Mr. Black," the man said with a bow and a twinkle in his eye. "Welcome to the Larson Estate."

They were ushered inside the beautiful building with all the fine furnishings, vaulted ceilings and many portraits hung on walls one might expect. It reminded Dorran of a grand museum.

Marcus opened the tall chestnut doors to the dining room, where, on the left side, a number of dishes sat along a fancy table covered with white linen. Dorran swallowed, rarely seeing so much food in one place: trays of low-fat yogurt, applesauce, bananas, oatmeal, lean poultry and fish, plain eggs, mashed potatoes, rice, noodles, white bread, juices and plain cereals. All the dishes that he could eat.

His eyes widened. "I don't think I'm *that* hungry."

Skye laughed and gave him a side hug. "Not just for you. That's another one of our changes: eating breakfast together with the staff every Saturday morning. Mother insisted."

Marcus led them to the dining table, where sat Adelaide Larson, next to a large number of the Larson staff: cooks, maids, gardeners and more, including their families. Adelaide stood and greeted Dorran with an enthusiastic hug before pointing out his seat next to hers.

"Today's breakfast is in your honor, Dorran!" she said. "We wish to welcome you as a member of our family." Her eyes shone as her words fazed Dorran.

He couldn't believe his ears. The Larsons were actually accepting him as a part of *their* family? He swallowed as his remaining preconceptions about rich people simply melted away.

"Thank you," he managed to say, as the staff clapped and vocally welcomed him.

Dorran and Skye were pushed to the front of the self-serving line, and although Dorran wasn't that hungry, he allowed Skye to fill his plate. The food was delicious, and he found himself eating much more than normal.

Conversation with the staff was pleasant, a few of them even sharing their own military experiences. Everyone was polite and seemed happy as they talked freely amongst themselves. Dorran met one of the housekeepers named Rosario, a gardener named Beth, and Jamie the chef.

Suddenly the doors to the dining room opened and closed and the staff rose to their feet.

Dorran turned to see a man walking toward them. He was older and carried himself proudly. He watched as the faces around him grew sober and their eyes dropped to the floor. Dorran stood, recognizing him as Mr. Larson, the CEO of Coeur d'Alene Bank & Trust, and owner of several companies around the country.

The man stopped and held out his hand to Dorran. He wore a slight smile.

"Welcome, Dorran," he said politely. "I am glad to finally meet you."

Dorran's eyes couldn't help but narrow as he looked first at Skye, and then at Charles Larson himself. Mixed feelings hit him, but he managed to take the hand and shake it firmly.

Charles Larson frowned. "It is possible that some of my preconceptions about others may not always be...accurate," he said. "Or so I have been told."

Dorran nodded, his face serious. "I am afraid the same is true with me," he said, looking the elder man in the eye. "There is nothing so expensive, really, as a big, well-developed, full-bodied preconception."

Charles Larson looked at him thoughtfully. "Yes. I think that E.B. White was certainly correct on that matter."

"Care to join us for breakfast, Father?" Skye asked, holding onto Dorran's right arm.

The man looked at her, his face turning sad.

"I certainly would if I could, my dear. But today's business is pressing, and I am unable to get away from it." He looked at Dorran. "However, I look forward to many conversations with you, young man."

Dorran tilted his head slightly. "As do I," he replied quietly. *Can this really be happening?* he asked himself. *Mr. Larson wants to have talks with me?*

Adelaide kissed her husband before he excused himself from the room, and everyone sat back down. But the nature call within Dorran was almost violent, and he made his way quickly to the bathroom. But by now his stomach turned sour and he felt shakes and cold sweats. Yet he hid it well, smiling as he returned to the meal.

From the conversation he heard between Skye, her mother and the staff, Charles Larson had never seemed upset about anything except his business misfortunes, until that morning when he could not stay for breakfast. Skye seemed excited along with everyone else until she looked at Dorran.

"Are you all right?" she asked quietly. "Your face is pale."

Dorran shrugged. "I think it's all the excitement. Stomach not having a good day."

"Why don't you two get some fresh air?" Adelaide suggested. "Out by the fountain there are some nice benches."

Dorran nodded as chills swept over him. "That sounds good."

But outside, Dorran only felt worse. His entire abdomen was like a raging volcano. He felt chilled to the bone and his energy level cratered, even with all the food he just ate. Skye led him as he slowly walked to a bench beside the beautiful red and black brick fountain, where she sat him down and held his hand. Marcus followed a short distance behind.

"I am sorry," Dorran said weakly. "I pictured our last outing far different than this."

"Yeah, me too," Skye said, her voice sounding disappointed. "But reality has a way of... of... Dorran?!"

Dorran closed his eyes and bent over, his pain too intense to bear any longer.

"That's it," Skye snapped. "I'm calling an ambulance."

Dorran opened his eyes and looked at her, shaking his head. "No ambulance," he groaned. "Can't afford it."

"Screw that!" Skye cried. "I don't care! We have to get you to the hospital!"

"Allow me to drive you, Dorran," Marcus offered, stepping forward. "You'll be there in no time."

"No health insurance," Dorran said. "Wait until I get to boot camp and see a doctor."

Skye huffed. "You won't make it to boot camp. Marcus, help me carry him!"

It was a short walk—no more than a hundred feet—but to Dorran it felt like five miles of pain. He inched along, supported by Skye and Marcus, as he remained doubled over from the raging lava within. After a moment of waiting against an entryway pillar, Marcus drove up and Skye helped him inside, where he lay, moaning.

Chapter 23
Fire

Skye sat in a waiting room of Coeur d'Alene General Hospital, surrounded by her mother, Sage, Olivia and Sidney. A few chairs over, Max and Finn sat, fidgeting with their cell phones.

It had been hours since Dorran was admitted to the ER. The doctors said they were still running tests while Dorran underwent anesthesia, but until now no one was able to give them information they did not already know.

Adelaide tried to be upbeat, assuring Skye repeatedly that they made it in time, the doctors and nurses were experts, and it was best to leave it to them.

But Skye felt angry. "You know what he said when I told him he was coming in?" she quietly said so Max couldn't hear. "He couldn't afford it because he had no health insurance! He would let himself...himself die before getting help?"

"Skye, he's here now," Sage said. "So it doesn't matter."

Adelaide shook her head. "Of course it doesn't. We will take care of the bills. He needn't worry about it." She looked at Skye's worried face. "And remember," she added. "No strings attached."

Skye hugged her mom in relief, feeling more tears flow down her cheeks.

Adelaide suddenly gasped and Skye turned her head. Walking toward them was Charles Larson, his face grim. But when he saw them, he tried to smile. He fumbled with his hands as he spoke.

"Yes, I had an important meeting today," he said, looking at Skye. "But as you are sometimes fond of saying, screw that!"

Skye leaped up and melted into the man's arms.

"I love you Father," she said quietly.

Chapter 24
Ice

Dorran woke in a hospital bed, with no stomach pain. No fevers or chills. No symptoms whatsoever. A male nurse stood by, taking his blood pressure.

"Good morning!" he said cheerfully.

But all Dorran could think about was boot camp and the deadline. Could he still make the flight in time? Would Skye drive him if he missed the bus?

"What day is it?" he asked in his morning groggy voice.

"Monday, August 3rd," he replied, matter-of-fact. "Are you feeling up for visitors? There's a small crowd waiting outside."

August 3rd? That sounded impossible. But if it was true, he'd likely be in deep trouble. Dorran glanced around his hospital room. Get Well balloons hung along the back wall and a variety of flowers bloomed at his bedside.

"Sure," he said. "And when can I leave?"

The man shrugged. "Only the doctor can tell you that."

Skye was the first who plowed through the door, literally running to his bed before stopping herself. Her face was all smiling tears as they embraced and kissed for several moments.

"I guess I missed my boot camp deadline," Dorran muttered after catching his breath.

Skye nodded proudly. "You sure did, soldier!"

"And that's a big negative on boot camp, soldier!" Trey said, as he stepped forward. As Max, Finn, and Brian and Lisa Parker walked up from behind, Trey waved a vanilla folder. "Apparently your father tried to join the military too."

Dorran sat up, wide-eyed. "My dad?"

Trey grinned. "Yep, about 23 years ago. But he had a medical condition called ulcerative colitis, and was discharged within a couple of months. And guess what? The doctors say you have it too. Sorry, bud, you can't be in the military with that condition."

Dorran was drowning in happy shock. "You're kidding."

Trey shook his head. "Not about something like this. Here's the proof." He dropped the folder on Dorran's chest. He sat up and quickly opened it. On the front of his application were stamped the words *Medical Discharge.*

"My superiors signed off on everything this morning."

"What about my physical?" Dorran asked, curious.

"They missed the signs." He shrugged. "Hey, it happens sometimes. I think they were more concerned about your past and present performance and so it didn't get noticed. And that's what my phone call was about. I had to dig up your record so they could proceed with the inquiry." He paused for effect. "So sorry, Dorran. You're out!"

"Thanks Trey!"

Trey winked. "Better luck next time."

Dorran felt as if he was floating on air, having the best dream imaginable. He looked at Skye, adoring her. He had his life back. He had her back. And he wouldn't have to wait two years for it.

"I'm not going to boot camp," he breathed happily.

Skye shook her head, her face filled with joy.

Dorran looked at Max. "Think I'll take a raincheck on my resignation."

"Duly noted and accepted!" Max said, coming forward and shaking Dorran's hand.

"But you and Skye should take some time off after you get patched up. Get away together on your bikes? Maybe tour? The shop will be fine without your services for a while."

Everyone agreed with that idea and started talking at once, laughing and suggesting all the places they would go.

Soon an elderly male doctor came in the room, greeted everyone, and checked on Dorran.

"Glad to have you back!" he said pleasantly. "As you've probably been informed, you do have ulcerative colitis, but fortunately we caught it in time. We started intravenous treatment, to which you are responding well so far. With any luck, you'll be out of here and on the road to recovery in a few days."

"No more ulcers?"

The man shook his head. "Not after your treatments."

"Thanks, Doc," Dorran said.

The man looked at him. "Don't just thank me. It was," and here he looked at a clipboard he held in his hands, "Charles Larson who made some phone calls, provided us with important information, and got things rolling for you. Without that, we might still be running tests!"

*

It was a beautiful, early September morning, around 48 degrees outside the Arrowroot Bakery. Dorran and Skye, packed and ready beside their bikes, hugged the small crowd of well-wishers goodbye. Adelaide Larson dabbed her wet eyes with a handkerchief as she kissed Skye and Dorran.

"Don't get lost in Canada!" Finn teased as he held Sage's hand.

"What fun is that?" Skye shot back good-naturedly.

Trey had his arms wrapped around Olivia. "Send us pictures on Instagram!" he said. "We want to know what Victoria is like."

"Will do," Dorran said as he slid his helmet on his head. Skye did the same, and after starting their bikes, they waved one last time and drove off into the beautiful sunrise.